not forever

not forever

alex mellanby

Matador
9 Priory Business Park,
Wistow Road, Kibworth Beauchamp,
Leicestershire. LE8 0RX
Tel: 0116 279 2299
Email: books@troubador.co.uk
Web: www.troubador.co.uk/matador
Twitter: @matadorbooks

ISBN 978 1800463 509

British Library Cataloguing in Publication Data.
A catalogue record for this book is available from the British Library.

Printed and bound in Great Britain by 4edge Limited
Typeset in 11pt Adobe Garamond Pro by Troubador Publishing Ltd, Leicester, UK

Matador is an imprint of Troubador Publishing Ltd

This book is dedicated to the children in terrible places who may not have the skills that Molly uses in this book. May we protect them.

The text could not have been written without the assistance of my wife Carolyn. Her expertise and knowledge were essential. Especially detailing the successes but sometime farcical errors that can be made in the system.

one

I am a girl who thought she could see forever, like a never-ending party game of grandmother's footsteps, always creeping up behind. Nat told me about forever and it's a game no one wants to play.

Shivering in a sun too weak for warmth, I don't want to care about forever or even later today. I want to stay sitting on this damp moss-covered stone. Mickey Mouse on my wrist says it's five more minutes, a few more if I don't mind the beating, thank you, Mickey.

Even though the rain has stopped, everything is dripping. Dartmoor doesn't know it should be summer and the sun has only just started to shine on the high peaks with just sheep and me for company. Wild and lonely, but in this last of sunlight the moor looks as though it has been washed clean. It is so beautiful, and I will save the picture in my stupid head, to keep the creeping thing away.

I turn for the house as Mickey ticks away. Was that a movement, above me, up among the rocks? A bird, a sheep, a shadow? Too late to look again. The whistle goes, more minutes than I should have taken. My best minutes have to be worth it.

I run, stumbling on clumps of grass, run faster, Molly, run like it's your last run because it might be that.

Ahead, the house. Lester and Mum call it our home. I don't. It's a shutdown house hidden in an overgrown tangle of trees and bushes. The walls could have been white once, now they're a slimy green with water running from a roof of cracked tiles. The windows are shut tight with ancient and peeling wooden shutters that keep everything in.

Once it must have been a posh house, high up on this moor, windows with a view for miles. Grand once and now no longer cared for. A lonely house with no neighbours near, no one to hear, no one to call. I race through the door, hoping he sees me hurrying and that will count against my stolen moments on the moor.

'Here she is,' Lester says without a trace of a smile. 'Now you can get off, Irene, get off down to the pictures with your friends.' He pockets the whistle that hauled me in and shows me his fist.

Tonight is Mum's night out. She has lots of those. Lester doesn't mind her going out, he sends her. Lester doesn't mind at all because he has his good girl with him. That's me, so he says, and he likes me near. For me, another planet would be too close.

Mum is small and skinny, me too. She's jumpy. I know that look means something bad is never far away. Her high heels and perfume don't hide the smell of fags or make her look like a mum. She doesn't have friends to take to the cinema. She doesn't go to the cinema at all and isn't always called Irene and is never much of a mother. She works at night, for cash. Why do they pretend? Pretending doesn't last long. Nothing here is make-believe.

Mum and I came to this moorland house after the last lot of trouble. Last stop East London. Before that, other towns, anywhere with dark narrow streets for Mum's nights out. Trouble seemed to arrive with anything that could give trouble. For me, it was not understanding and refusing to understand and never wanting to come anywhere near to understanding.

I was given a new label. One of the women in our London room gave it to me.

'Make a good turn with a girl like that, a real asset.' I don't remember her name, just her face screwed up as she sucked the life out of her weed-filled smoke.

After that, Mum called me her little asset, not her daughter. Her little asset, she says and tells me not to grow up too quickly. She negotiates my age with the other woman.

'Could get away with nine,' Weed-sucker says.

'You reckon?' Mum looks at me. I'm what you might call "scraggy".

'She's got a lovely little face,' Weed says. 'They'd love that.'

I thought she was being nice. I don't know exactly how old I am. 'Impossible,' you say? I have birth certificates, I've seen them. Mum knows people who can get you nearly anything. Now I have one that says I'm nine years old, birthday in March, whatever.

I told Mouse I was meant to be nine because mum loves her baby girl. Mouse said it's because younger assets are more valuable. I told Mouse to shut up. I tell a lot of people to shut up. Like the other children sharing our space in London. They liked to tell you how bad everything will be and how it was always best to hate in silence and not to think. It is the sort of thing that Mouse often said to me in my head. I tried not to listen to Mouse. It didn't work.

'We need a nice place.' Mum puffed through the constant sweet smell of homegrown hash, it made her calmer, but she wasn't good at planning. We stayed in a flat of women and children and a baby, sharing beds in shifts to match our mothers' working days – or nights. I liked the idea of a nice place; I could understand that. I had flowers and sheep in mind.

We were left alone most of the time in the flat.

'Education by telly,' one of the women said, switching channels until an animal programme came on. 'Best you learn this,' she laughed and walked away. Not a happy laugh.

Nat was our boss. 'Fuck that,' she said and turned back to *Saw IV*. Natalie was an older girl who knew everything and told us about it. Sometimes Nat would go out with the women. She told us about that too. She'd throw things at us when she got angry. Mouse had to hide.

Sometimes Nat would turn off the telly and tell us things we didn't want to hear. Nat told me about fucking. I didn't believe her. I mean why would anyone want to do that? Nat said they paid my mum to do it. That she'd been fucked by so many men no one would know who my dad might be. I cried about that. Like Nat cried most nights in her sleep.

I asked Nat how old she thought I was.

'Can't be more than twelve,' she said. 'Not started bleeding, have you?'

I shook my head. I knew what she meant, not everything but enough to know it had to be bad when it happened.

o

There was a lot of talk and nothing changed until something from someone else's real world made it happen. Even in those dark streets our life here couldn't last. Maybe someone decided they didn't like the look of us, not that anyone ever would come close to liking us. A gobby woman turned up at the front door. Nat was told to keep us quiet. The woman left after an argument. She said she'd be back.

Mum said we had to run from Mrs Gobby who was one of the "social". Everyone knew the social put you away in a dark hole and never let you out. Why could that be any worse than what was happening anyway? But it wasn't my decision to make, never was.

We ran, or at least got out of the flat in the middle of the night with the rest of everyone before the men knew anything about us leaving. Not exactly a lot of packing to do. Just working clothes and whatever chemicals Mum could snatch. I have a small pink bag on my back, that was snatched too. Mouse is in a pocket. I wanted her to look out, but I think it's dangerous.

Victoria Bus Station in the early morning, there were others not wanting to talk. But we were off to our "nice place". I whistled. Mum told me to shut it.

Mum showed me a leaflet on the bus. Pictures of Devon with cows and fields and happy children playing. She said she knew someone there who would help. She actually said, 'To hide,' but I decided to miss that. Leaving London, I did see cows and sheep and fields. Not so much the children playing, I guess they were at school.

'When can I go to school?' I asked. She doesn't reply to that sort of question and I don't ask twice because it seems to annoy her, tells me not to be stupid. Three times is a slap. Mum went to sleep.

With Mum asleep I pulled Mouse up from the pocket in my bag, her nose was quite dirty. I showed her the leaflet, I think she liked it. I whispered to her, told her all the things about our nice place. I don't think she believed me. That made me cross and I poked her back down into the bag. What did she know? She was only a toy. A little later I whispered, 'Sorry.'

We arrived in rain. Different to London, smelt better, looked a simple place. Quieter. Mum led the way. I tried another whistle, but my mouth was too dry. We stopped at the toilet.

'Nice place isn't it?' she said, not waiting for an answer and I don't think she meant the loo, which smelt like any other one. 'Got to look right.' She pulled out stuff from her bag. So that even after the five-hour bus journey and the rain I looked sweet, a pretty little girl, dressed prettily by her mother. My hair was long and brushed. That's one thing Mum did for me, quite a lot. I think it made her feel good, brushing my hair. Kept me looking young, she said.

The leaflet from the bus had a map of the town. 'Down there.' Mum points. I wondered how she knew. Had she been here before? She hadn't told me that, hadn't told me that she knew of this place before we arrived. Made me think and imagine that this could be alright, stupid idea.

Mum took us to a park by a river and the rain had nearly stopped, which seemed the best it ever did in this small grey town. There had to be better parks than this one, with its broken seesaw and a swing without seats. It wasn't somewhere that mothers brought their children. It was more the sort of place for older children to cause trouble on their own.

'We'll be alright here.' Mum looked around. She said she had a gift for finding the right people.

We sat on a bench; Mum dried it with something from her bag, not very dry. Mum left a gap.

'Why are we here?' I moved a little closer to her.

'Stay there.' She pushed me back.

I swung my legs, kicked them in the air. Mum slapped them down. 'Keep still, will you.'

Not long before Lester passed by, twice, checking and each time Mum nodded at him until he was hooked. I didn't like him. Lester frightened me from the first second I saw him. His face was pudgy. Like a bowl of angry mashed potato with lumps. He frightened me in the park, he frightened me as we moved into the dingy café.

Mum had been more vague about this than usual, which meant she'd told me nothing.

Lester said he had a house. 'Lovely place, quiet as anything, neighbours won't be a bother.' He seemed a little breathless as he spoke, almost panting. His eyes moved over me. Mum told me to smile for Mr Lester. She'd taught me how to smile when you don't want to do anything other than scream.

'Buy you some hot chocolate,' he said.

I didn't want hot chocolate. I wanted to go to our nice place alone with Mum. But Mum was holding my arm so tight it hurt and whispering for me to 'watch it', which meant I would have to like hot chocolate.

I had a mug of something that wasn't hot and didn't taste like chocolate. 'They only had tea,' Lester said when he saw my face.

'Say thank you, Mol,' Mum told me. I mumbled.

Lester said he had an aunt who died. Well, nearly died, he added and sounded confused. 'Nearly died and left me her house.'

That didn't make sense, even to me who does her best not to understand. But I didn't ask Mr Lester – I never remember him telling us his name, Mum just knew it. I didn't ask him to explain how his aunt died and then not died.

'She's in hospital.' Lester felt he had to say more. 'She doesn't want any visitors if anyone asks.' He had trouble talking, as though he couldn't take a big enough breath. His words came in panted gasps, he was fidgeting, looking around him, looking at the door. 'Can we go?' There's a change in his voice that I will recognise.

Mum nodded. We left.

My mind clears from that first day and any hope of what could have been my nice place.

o

Tonight is still Mum's night out.

She calls from the door, out of sight, ''Bout time you came in, Mol, out all day on that moor, you be a good girl for your dad.'

I listen, hoping one day I will hear something new, but there's nothing new. I try to pretend she doesn't know, doesn't know what it is her asset has to do to keep us here.

Lester grabs me by the hair. I know not to call out.

'Bye, then,' Mum calls and shuts the door.

I expect it, but don't see the blow to the side of my head, biting my lip as I go down, hitting my elbow. I'm not fat enough to soften the fall. It always starts like this. We still haven't heard the car pull away. Mum could come back, but she won't. It's a distance she has to drive not to go to the cinema.

'I told you to get in by five, didn't I?' Lester tries to snarl. I know he wants to sound frightening, but he has a squeaky voice every time this starts. Even though I know what is going to happen it's difficult not to laugh at his voice. I can see he knows that.

I say nothing. I hurt. The car goes. The kick is harder. I hurt more.

'Didn't I tell you that?' The squeak is louder.

'Yes,' I mumble, too quietly for him.

I have no fight in me, I have given up trying to be myself. But please don't cry, Molly, even though that is what he wants.

He walks away to his end of the kitchen, waving for me to follow.

'Are you going to be a good girl?' he says, and we start the dance as he removes his belt and swigs from the bottle.

'Come and make me happy.'

My mind is on the move, I'm out onto the moor. I see Steeperton in the distance, the pointed tor with something on top, looks like a box, I will go there one day. My smile is fixed, Lester's noise is gross, but I have my picture. I trace the stream along the valley, the little bridge, the rush of water, some other walkers with huge backpacks, off to walk so very far. I join them until they disappear from view. Lester grunts, piggy grunts. I could hide in the purple heather, hide forever. I want to run down to the stream and wash, lie in the tumbling water, let it flush the Lester away, but now he wants his fucking tea.

I'm the good girl. Now he wants his fucking tea. I heat up pizza with anchovies and a trickle of snot that I place in the middle, not so good girl. And a sprinkle of something Mum gave me. I stand and wait, wait on Lester, wait for scraps. There aren't many of them, but I'm not keen on snot. I lose the moor as the sights and smells of stale cigarettes and whisky take over in the darkness of this shuttered room, the partly dead aunt's room.

'What you looking at?' he slurs. The squeak has gone.

There is a list of how I must not reply to that. Don't say 'nothing', 'cos he says, 'you say I'm nothing?' before he hits me. Don't say 'don't know', because he says, 'I'll teach you to know' before he hits me. Nothing I say matters because he hits me anyway. What happened didn't make him happy.

'I'll teach you to be a good girl,' he says while he lands a punch, but this time it isn't hard, his face has slipped, the mashed potato lines of his face are turning to mush. He's not happy and there's something else in this disgusting man's face. As though he's lost.

He won't make me any sort of good. He will teach me to be a very bad girl. I know that. That's the forever when I'm a bad girl. That's what I'll be. I'll grow up bad and hating everyone. I can feel it, the hate, until the pain of this last beating should make me cry.

'Get out,' Lester mumbles a shout. I can hear that he is trying to find himself again. 'Get to your room and no noise.'

He watches me shuffle away and tries to laugh, but only a half-laugh because even though I can barely stagger away, I didn't cry. Or at least not enough. I make for the room I've been given. Nowhere near Mum, just off the kitchen down a musty corridor.

I want the bathroom, but it is back past the kitchen. I'm not allowed to use it unless he's out, best not to think of what I have to do. For now, I snuffle down under a quilted thing that smells like a wet dog, but it might just be the smell of an old person, like an old aunt. I often check to make sure she is not still in here.

I wrap myself in the ancient bed clothes and I hope that the sprinkle of something Mum gave me to put on his pizza keeps him quiet for the night. She said all good girls need a little help. I try not to hate Mum but it's hard. Lester snores while I count sheep grazing on far away hills.

I count more sheep until I hear the car returning in the early light. It's not safer then but I sleep until the shouting starts. Mum gets a smack in Lester's hangover morning, before he leaves.

Lester works at a garage. Not the one outside this house, somewhere else. I heard him on the phone, and I don't believe he likes the work but has to go. There's someone even more awful that calls him in. It's not a normal garage.

I want to cry. But I don't. I plan my walk for tomorrow. The moor. Can it hide the forever?

two

On that first day of Lester, we left the café and the park as it was getting dark, off in his car, stinking of fags and booze and something else I tried not to recognise. I was in the back with the rubbish and the other smell. He bought chips.

I wanted to believe we were going to the "nice place" I had built for myself on the bus from London. The leaflet started me off. I pictured children playing around our cottage, pictured me playing.

'Shut it, Mol,' Mum turned to me with a loud whisper and turned back to say something to Lester which I didn't hear.

I'd been talking aloud to Mouse without realising it. Mouse has been with me for ages. I found her in the London flat. Most of us found things in the stuff that was left for us assets. Some found dolls and bears and action men. I found a mouse, a yellowish-grey stuffed mouse with a purple hat – now lost. She still had her whiskers. I wanted to get her another hat.

'Shh,' I hissed to Mouse, poked her down into the pocket and pulled the zip to make sure she was safe. I had to keep Mouse safe. Nat would have pulled the head off anything she caught you playing with. Nat didn't play at children's games; she'd say that and turn away.

o

Daylight dimmed that sooty grey you get as we drove up lanes brushing against hedgerows, sloshing through puddles, passing old houses, windows with yellow lights, and up higher again. Lester revving the engine as we only just made the hill and swearing at his useless windscreen wipers with the rain much heavier. I was losing any idea of my "nice place" in Lester's car.

Mum sat on the edge of her seat, jerking her head from side to side. She always has a knife in her handbag. She kept feeling for it and I wanted to tell her to stop before Lester saw what she was doing. She turned and flicked me a nod. I knew to check out the door handles and get ready to run. Mum's told me enough times what to do. Her plan.

The Plan: Mum pulls out the knife, I jump out and run around to bang on the driver's window, get him to look at me – time for Mum to escape. It's the plan we'd use in town with people about. We weren't in a town, we weren't anywhere, no people. The plan wouldn't work, wouldn't work anywhere. Stupid idea. I never wanted to need a plan like that. I could feel my tummy squeeze as I went over and over it in my head. I just knew I'd trip or something stupid.

If Mr Lester had decided to kill us, then he would have found it easy. That's what I thought when he turned into a narrow gap between two walls, almost no space to open the doors. Was Mum just going to stab him, was that the new plan? I held my breath. Mum didn't move, nothing happened. Lester wasn't going to kill us; it would be much worse than that.

'Lovey.' Lester screwed round to me in the back. 'Get the garage door.'

We'd stopped, and through streaming rain the headlights picked out a garage with one of those lift-up doors. I looked at Mum and she nodded so I edged my way out.

The rain was pissing down. I was drenched as I struggled with the rusty bent metal door and waited for Lester to drive in. He told us to keep the noise down.

'Don't want to disturb anyone in the village.' Lester pinched my cheeks hard enough to hurt.

I wanted to lean in and press the horn, see if anyone did notice, because I couldn't see it happening. No one was going to come out in this rain to check what was happening to Mum and me. No one would have checked on us even if it had been a bright shiny summer's day. Not when they'd got a look at us. Might have called the police though and I guessed that's why Lester wanted us quiet. It was his "nice place".

We ran from the garage up slimy steps thick with weeds. Lester let us in, his hand through a broken pane in the glass door. Hadn't his aunt given him a key? Inside bare lightbulbs and a musty wet smell. No one to welcome us, no one else lived here.

Lester slumped down in a chair. I didn't know what sort of room we were in. Grubby. On one side a grease-stained window over a sink of unwashed mugs and plates and stuff, kitchen units from before the ice age, a cooker that looked far too dangerous to use. Four hard brown wooden chairs had been pulled up to a wooden table.

Lester, at the other end, had settled in a saggy armchair next to a fireplace with no fire. Next to him, his bed, a mattress on the floor and bedclothes unmade and soiled. I didn't like the way Lester kept looking at the bed. Looking at me. He'd found a bottle of something which he kept swigging – no glass.

'Nice,' Mum said with her hand still in her handbag.

'Take a look around.' Lester waved his arms as though he owned the place although it looked like this might be the only room he used.

'Business first.' Mum moved him to the table. They sent me to look around while they talked over money and drugs. Mum was negotiating, Lester was talking with his squeaky voice. She told him that we would be good for him, how much we could do for him.

I didn't go far. A hallway led off the kitchen and into the dark. There were noises, creaks, groans and banging. I wasn't looking around here on my own. I stood by the door. I didn't listen, I tried not to listen. Because I had a bad feeling about what Mum was negotiating. I went back in. No one looked guilty.

'Bring me my bag.' Mum got up, pointing.

I handed over her cheap holdall with stuff we had brought from London. She put something into the bag and her hands were shaking. She led me out of the room.

'Don't take long,' Lester's voice crumbled.

There weren't many bulbs working. Mum went up the stairs using her phone to light the way. It was a work phone and hadn't rung in this new house, yet. We creaked on bare wooden steps. I was going slowly with Mum being jittery and I knew it wasn't because of Lester. She needed a fix. She found another bedroom, stripped bare except for a single bed with a striped stained mattress that sagged badly in the middle. Old blankets on the floor.

Mum sat to search her handbag, she looked up. 'Get downstairs and watch him.'

She needed the drugs and not me. What was I meant to watch for? I didn't want to go but I didn't want to stay while she gave herself the hit because after that she wasn't really there anyway.

'You be a good girl for him, eh?' she called as I reached the door and she wasn't waiting for an answer, that was my only instruction. Did I ever really manage to pretend Mum had no idea what was happening, what she'd let me in for? What sort of man Lester was? She must have met him in London on one of her nights on the street. So, Lester was the nice sort of man who was going to put us up in his house, and for what? I left her getting out her drug stuff and slowly went back down in the dark, trying to believe her words meant something different.

'Like it?' Lester slurred.

I nodded with my practised smile.

'Where's your mum?' he asked, but he knew.

'Upstairs,' I muttered.

'Did she tell you to be a good girl?'

I nodded.

'Know what that means?'

I didn't want to know then, still don't.

'Thought so.' Lester knocked me to the floor before he explained everything that a good girl has to do.

He pulled me up to hit me, holding my stupid dress by the neck, his hand twisting it tight. When I tried to look away, he hit me. When I tried to do anything, he hit me. When I did nothing, he hit me. He smacked me around the head until my ears rang and I couldn't hear his words so then he punched my tummy and I doubled up while he laughed.

I tried to make out what I could do that didn't make him hit me before I realised it was his game and he wanted to hit me, nothing I could do to stop it. When he did stop hitting me it got so much worse.

Mum didn't reappear. When Lester had finished with me, he turned away as though he didn't want to see my face. I didn't know what to do, what did he want?

'Get out,' he shouted at the wall and when I didn't move, 'Get OUT. Get down there.' He waved his arm behind his back, towards another door. 'GO.'

I limped out with my backpack. There was only one other room in the corridor leading from the kitchen. It was completely dark. I flicked on the lamp with no shade. A bed stood in the corner, some blankets on the floor. I turned out the light and sat with blankets wrapped around me and I watched the door. I hurt, everything seemed to hurt, but I didn't want to see how bad it was, I didn't want to look at myself, I never wanted to touch myself again. And I shivered, shaking all over even though it wasn't really cold.

But it had stopped, he hadn't killed me.

It had stopped and I was alone. It had stopped, and I didn't understand why that became so very important. I felt I had escaped. He hadn't killed me. Nat had told me all – and I mean ALL – the things that men could do to you. That man hadn't done them all. Had I escaped?

That man with his squashy face and squeaky voice had wanted me, to hurt me over and over, to do the things that Nat had told me men will do. He was desperate. He wanted me until it was over, then he didn't.

I wanted to talk to someone, I didn't want to talk, I never wanted to see anyone again. Mouse was still in my pink bag. I hadn't taken her out. I didn't want to talk to her. She'd know I was disgusting. Nobody would ever want to be with me again, nobody would want me again. What had I done wrong?

Was that it? Had I been swapped for a load of drugs? Was it once or was this really forever? Surely it was just once? I didn't want to move. I didn't want to find the rest of me, it wasn't me under the blanket. I didn't want to touch it. I pulled Mouse out and stuck her under the pillow, I did it quickly before she got a chance to ask anything.

As the minutes passed, I could not get Lester out of my head, of what he had done to me. I wanted to stop thinking about him or anything. I couldn't. There was nothing else. I wasn't me anymore, I didn't belong to me anymore. I heard him snoring. I had to find Mum.

Tiptoe. At each step I felt my stomach heave. I made the hall. I sped up the stairs, catching my toe in the dark but I made no noise at all. Into Mum's room. She snored loudly, like him. She was sprawled across the bed with one leg hanging over the side and a blanket half-covering her.

I snuggled in, warm.

'Mmmm,' she breathed, turned over, woke. 'What the fuck?' She shoved me out of the bed so hard that I tumbled onto the floor. 'Piss off.' She turned back to snoring.

On the floor there was nothing. I stayed there for ages, but it was so cold and hard that I had to move in the end. I crawled to the door. A look back at Mum, she was out of it, still snoring. I wanted to get back into the bed; I couldn't. With a little light in the sky, I crept back the way I had come. Down the stairs and a shaking tiptoe past him, not looking, pretending he wasn't there but knowing he was. Back to the room he'd sent me to. My head was swimming, so tired. I must have slept.

I heard voices in the kitchen. I think Mum was talking about the weather, ordinary stuff. I was still on the bed. I didn't think of what had happened. I wanted it all to be ordinary.

This could be an old lady's room; it could even have been someone's aunt's room. I was perched on a high single bed pushed up against the wall. Above me old pots and jars of half-pulled out rubbish on the edge of a shelf. An ancient picture on the wall that might have been animals, but it was too grubby to see what they were. Everything seemed brown and faded and dark. One window, high up on the wall, was too high to see out unless I stood on a chair. Even if I did that, I didn't think I'd see much because there was a mass of bushes right up against the glass.

Mouse was still under the pillow, hidden, but I wouldn't talk to her. If I talked to her it would make it real, if I didn't then I could pretend. Pretending didn't really work, but it was all I had.

I think Lester must have searched this room, things from an old set of drawers were pulled out and on the floor. Perhaps his aunt didn't leave a list of her possessions. I don't think Lester would have found anything that he wanted. It was a mess of old clothes. I wasn't going to tidy it up. This wasn't my home.

The talking in the kitchen became louder. Did I hear Mum saying she was going out? Was she leaving me, leaving me with him? I crept out to listen. I heard her asking for the car keys. Standing behind the kitchen door to Lester's room, I was shaking. I had a blanket around me, underneath the remains of clothes that did not hide what he had done.

'Hello Molly.' Lester pulled open the door, fast, and he tousled my hair. 'Don't you go listening behind doors,' he turned away. 'Get you into trouble,' he added, as if I wasn't in enough.

Mum tried to give me a hug. That hurt and I pushed her away. She chucked me another dress before she left. I was standing in the middle of the room holding it with my mouth open. What did I have to do?

'Can you cook, Molly?' he said, with a smile.

Smiles on mashed potato face, him rustling my hair. Right then I would have swapped anything to keep him like that. Of course I could cook, wash, sweep the house, whatever, anything that could stop him from… just keep him happy in a different way.

He wanted eggs for breakfast, cooked just perfectly on fried bread. There was only just enough for him, so I hoped the stuff Mum had been sent to get wasn't just drugs. If she did come back at all.

Keeping him eating was a victory, almost making me happy, normal. I was jumping at any sound, too keen to wash up. He talked about his garage while he ate, the things he was going to do with all the money he would make, which sounded unlikely. I tried to say something but absolutely no sound came from my mouth.

After breakfast the smiling stopped.

'You can stop washing up.' He grabbed me by the hair and pulled me over his knee. And talked. Each sentence with a slap across my bum.

'Being my good girl is our secret. If you say anything to anyone, you're dead,' he said, but sounded anxious and still squeaked in this talk. 'Dead, you hear?'

I guessed he knew that dead sounded better than what was happening to me alive, so he came up with the other threat.

'But I won't kill you until I've broken your ma.' He pointed to a heavy iron poker. 'You talk or try to get away and I'll smash her legs so bad she'll never walk again, just crawling around begging. Do you hear? It will be your fault.'

My answer had to be like a play, his play, and we played it over and over:

I say: yes.
He says: yes what?
I say: yes, it will be my fault.
And?
I won't talk.
Why won't you talk?
I won't talk because I'm a good girl.

It was a talk we were often going to have, a script I had to learn. I believed him, he'd smash Mum's legs with his poker if I talked or ran off. The thing is that I thought he was going to do that sometime anyway, whatever I did. Most of my head told me to run, now. It's Mum's fault we were here, her fault why I was here. Why do I care if Lester smashed her to pieces? I thought about it, couldn't do it.

When he'd finished beating me, I was thrown to the ground.

'I knew you'd be a good girl.' It's a matter of fact voice he used. 'We'll have lots of fun, won't we?'

On the floor, I couldn't think of an answer. Fun? We'd have lots of fun, he'd said. Really?

'Won't we?' he almost spelled the words.

'Yes,' I mumbled.

'Yes, WHAT?' He risked a daylight shout.

'Yes Daddy.' I used the words he had taught me.

'I'll be outside,' he told me before he picked up the iron poker from the fire. 'This is the one I'll use to break her bones.' He let out a little laugh and smacked it into his hand. 'So you just stay here and clean up a bit.'

He left. I breathed again, in gasps. I ached with bruises, I retched with something foul and hot coming from my empty guts. And then I hated. I was nearly there. Forever hating is so easy when you have someone to hate. Nothing to take away the worst hate. Because the thing I hated more than anything was myself.

Lester came back.

'I don't think I'll bother going out today.'

three

The house is creaking like it could fall apart. Someone is knocking loudly. I jerk awake. I am not ready for this. Am I meant to be ready? What for? Please, no. All of me tightens up and that hurts. But I am alone. I look up and the noise is just the wind banging a plant against the glass. This house needs some fixing. If I put my hand up to the window, I can feel wind coming through the cracks.

I hear Mum call, 'Bye Moll, see you later. Lester's in the garage.' She's gone again.

I want to disappear. To vanish, to be so small that no one can see me, and when I mean no one it is Lester who must not see me. Any second he can appear. He doesn't have to be in the room for me to shiver like there is an icicle inside of me. I must try to look around. I need to find an escape, but I must hide it if I find it. I can't let on that's what I'm doing.

If Mum has gone out, she might not come back. That happened in London, she disappeared for three days. There were other people around in London. Here, there's only Lester.

Today I think he has really gone out, but only to his own garage. It's another place where he does something. I don't think he does real work. I want him to go there too because I think it scares him. I have no idea what happens there. I just hope it is really bad, maybe he could get killed. I shouldn't try to imagine that happening, it is just stupid imagination. I just don't feel strong enough to come up with real ideas, like what to do next.

I can hear sounds from outside because Lester's garage is near my window. I'm not getting up to look. If I see him, it will all come back, in my head I will see it all again. Thinking of him seeing me stops my breathing, something happens in the middle of me, I don't know what it is. I have to find a way to make this go away. It's not much different from imagining making Mum different. I hate myself, but I imagine making him happy, not his sort of happy, normal happy, then he might stop.

Breathe again, Molly. What can I do to stop this? Nothing. Mum's not going to help, she got us here. Can I find something in the house, to kill him? Could I do that? No, but I must try. No matter how it hurts. Breathe, Molly. Should I take Mouse? She would make me braver. Can't take Mouse, haven't told Mouse what has happened to me. When I do tell Mouse, it will make it real, even though it is real anyway.

Alone, I tiptoe through the kitchen, past the bathroom and into the empty hallway leading down to a front door that looks like it's never used, partly covered with an old piece of curtain with a broken chair leaning against it. This place smells old. The walls must have been painted once, now they're coloured, yellowed like fag-stained fingers. Below the paint are brown wooden panels, peeling, and some look rotten as though the water has crept into the house through all the cracks. It smells damp as well and still the wind is almost screaming outside.

There's nothing here, bare walls and wooden floorboards. If it's Lester's relative, she took everything with her – if she isn't dead and buried in the garden. Maybe Lester sold everything after killing her.

There are two old heavy doors off the hall. I try to open one, but it's locked or jammed. I try the handle on the other one, it swings open and crashes into the wall, swings back and then crashes again. I grab to hold it, to make the noise stop. I screw my eyes tight shut and listen; my breathing has stopped again. The wind is so loud I won't hear him coming. But he will have heard me.

I look back towards the kitchen. I feel him coming, I see his face, twisted, angry. I shake and want to run but I can't. I stumble forward and slide to the floor, leaning against the noisy door. The places he has hit me ache and I wait for more pain when he finds me. I open my eyes a bit at a time, better not to see all of him at once. There is nothing. Stupid me. Stupid frightened me. I want to try again. I gulp at the air.

This room is an empty draughty space that echoes with the wind. A huge bush has grown right over the windows so it's almost dark and its branches hit the glass like someone trying to get in. There's one old and broken armchair but no other furniture, no carpet.

You can see where there must have been pictures on the wall, now just cleaner square marks on the peeling walls. An old stone fireplace on one side with soot spilling from the grate. It must have blown down the chimney, doesn't look like anyone's had a fire here for ages.

I crawl towards the chair. Leaving the door, it slams shut behind me. I jump again. I cannot stop myself believing Lester has followed me into the room. I turn. He must be there. I wait for the blow. There's no one there but that doesn't make it any better. He's just outside and he will come in sometime. Even if I could get out of the house I have nowhere to go, no one to go to.

I leave the big room to go back into the hall and find the stairs. I take a step. Why am I doing this? I know this is worse. If he catches me upstairs, I know he'll hurt me. That's what he likes doing. I won't stop looking, he will hurt me anyway, so I might as well go on. That's too brave a thought, but I still go on. There are more doors on the landing, more mostly empty rooms.

Mum must have found a few other bits of furniture which she's dragged into her room, a chair, some sort of small cupboard. Where did she find them, because there's nothing in the other rooms? Makes me wonder why there's still stuff in the room I have to use.

This house is not just empty, it's stripped of everything. I walk into the middle of one room on old wooden floorboards that crack as I stand on them with a noise like a firework going off. That squashes any last bits of being brave out of me. There's no point in being found up here, there's nothing I can see which will help me, so I rush – which means hobble – downstairs and back to the room I've been told is mine. Nothing here is anything I want, nothing's mine, not even me.

I slump back on the bed. At least the wind seems to have dropped.

I could have done all sorts of things. I do wonder about setting fire to the place. The fire brigade could rescue me. Would Lester break Mum's legs if he couldn't prove it was me? I think he wouldn't care about proof. I also think there might not be a fire brigade near here. I could turn on the gas and blow us up – oh – no gas, it's all electric. I spend ages on thoughts like this. Nothing good and time is going slowly. I look out of my door again. No sounds.

Back away from the kitchen my room is in a muddy sort of corridor, another door at the end with glass panels which are totally dirty. I had looked at the door before. In my mind it's my escape door and I didn't want to go near it in case it disappears. I don't mean really disappears, but Lester could just move me to another room, nail up the door or whatever. He's probably done the nailing up already.

I decide to use my luck up and look at it properly. In the muddy corridor there are rows of pegs and old coats with pairs of welly boots underneath. I can see at least five pairs of boots and more stuck in a cupboard. Must be the old lady's stuff, nothing that Lester would wear, too small. Why is this stuff here when the rest of the house is empty? I sniff one of the coats, don't know why, maybe I wondered if I could smell the old lady. I don't think I can, some smell I can't recognise. I like it.

She must have done a lot of walking. The boots are well-worn and when I look into the cupboard it's not just wellies, she had some tough-looking walking boots. All of this smells the same, what is it? And where did she go walking?

I move slowly to the door I want to be mine. Obviously, it's locked. The only way out of the house is straight past the garage, straight past him. On the window ledge there's a rusty mark that looks like it's where the key was kept, Lester probably has it. I search for another key. Nothing hidden in the boots or coats. I think back to the room I've been given, to the pots and jars.

I search everything. I find broken pencils, marbles, pieces

of string. I am starting to panic, breathing fast and feeling faint. I find a tin of keys that has slid behind the bed or perhaps been hidden there? I know that time must run out on me, I've been left alone too long. I still have to try. I take the tin back to the door. I think I will know which key it is because I want it to be my special door. But that doesn't happen; I try the lot, and there are at least twenty keys in this tin, before I find the right one.

The door lock creaks and rasps, and I stop and wait for silence. I close it. I walk away. Can I hear Lester in the garage? I don't know, so I go back down the corridor to my special door and listen. No sound. I open my door and look out. The smell hits me, something fresh. I have only seconds because there's a crash back in the kitchen.

'Moll.' I hear Mum's voice. 'Moll, come here, lunch.'

The door won't shut. Another crash and Lester shouts something. I lean against the door and I'm talking to God. I tell him I'm not really bad. I'll do anything he wants. God suddenly becomes Lester in my head. The door closes, I turn the lock.

'Moll, where are you?' Mum's voice cracks. She's scared. The sort of scared you might make if the man in the same room had picked up the poker.

'Coming,' I shout and try to run. I have to get there before he breaks her legs.

There aren't any broken legs. Mum's on her own. I see Lester closing the door, going out, back to the garage I suppose. Mum has pizza, that's my lunch and she has a Napolitano.

'Why?' I point at the anchovies. Complaining is the first normal thing I've done. Back to normal, me complaining, then Mum shouting at me. That's normal, and I want more of it because it's as near to getting away from here as I think will ever happen. At least Mum shouting at me means I am a real child for a moment.

Mum just shrugs.

I guess the anchovies came with the free pizza, free as in someone else's. We both pick them out, before I just pick. The food, and everything here makes me feel sick.

Does Mum believe this is normal, her and me having lunch? She's going on about things like the weather, mess in the bathroom, the smell of Lester's car. As if she thinks mothers should go on about that sort of stuff. As if being here, moving in with that man, is a natural thing to do. I want something very different. I want to hear how we get out of this place. I'd like to hear how she's going to kill Lester and then we live here happily ever after. I can feel myself getting angry but there's no point. And it does feel a bit normal having Mum here with me for a while. I like to hear her talking. Asking questions will just start her shouting and then Lester will come in. So I let her go on.

As she does, I can see something else changing her. I nod and smile and agree with everything she says. I want to keep this normal bit of her. It doesn't work. Her hands are starting to shake and she's drifting, making less sense. She pokes the pizza and says she needs to lie down. That's not what she means. She doesn't need a bed. She needs a candle, spoon and a syringe. We speak in codes. Like Mum saying I have to be a good girl doesn't mean I have to go to school and do my best.

She's gone.

I scrape pizza and anchovies into the bin. Overflowing bin. I start to wash up the pile of mess in the sink. Might things change if I'm helpful? Could this ever be a normal family?

Washing up is sort of normal so I carry on. The window in front of me is filthy with grease and other dirt. I scrape a bit of a hole to look out. I can't see much because of the overgrown trees and bushes that come right up to the weather-cracked windowsill. Just mess out there in the garden.

A cold feeling creeps up on me. What else is out there in the garden? Has Lester really killed the old lady and buried her out there in the dirt? Is that going to happen to me? Bits of pizza come back up in my mouth, I swallow, I won't make a mess. I have to move away but I can't make it back to my room, so I sit by the table. I need to get out into the air. I can't use my special door. I use the other one, Lester's door.

'What you want?' Lester magically appears and smacks me over the head. 'Don't you come wandering out here. I'm busy.'

I need the air, but I need to escape from him. I dodge another blow to get back inside but trip and hurt my shoulder.

Lester laughs, 'That'll teach you.'

Back inside I sit on one of the hard chairs. Words string together in my head, words I want to scream out loud, dangerous words to scream at Lester, too dangerous to even say in a whisper. But most of all I want to say it won't teach me, because teaching is what happens to ordinary little girls in school, not when they're being knocked around. I have been to school once or twice and while it wasn't great I could cope with the bullying, kids of my own age. I could deal with that, until they excluded me.

Too much. It's too much right now. I have to do something. I see Lester's bottle on the table. My hand edges towards it, I grab it by the neck. *Don't*, I hear myself think, but it's too late. I hurl his whisky bottle to the wall; through the crash of broken glass, I see the yellow liquid trickling down the paintwork, slowly reaching the floor. I cannot stop. I stand and kick the chair. At the sink I throw everything I find. Plates and glasses break on another wall. I kick the bin and all the mess flies out, anchovies skid across the floor. I kick again.

Lester and Mum arrive.

Mum's not going to help. I see her drooping eyes, the glazed look she has after her drug fix. Lester has an eye-popping crazy look as he sees the broken bottle. I run at him, my fists whirling, it's hopeless. He lifts me into the air and I'm flying. Towards the wall. I think I may be dead and that isn't so bad. But I'm not. My eyes open and Lester's coming for me.

Mum tries to get between us. 'Don't,' she cries. 'Don't. She'll be a good girl, won't you, Molly?'

Mum gets knocked out of the way. Then he's on me and I get the kicks. His heavy boots crash into whatever part of me they find. I'm not moving, just moaning. He stops when I'm too broken to even moan. He's at the door swearing and shouting at me, telling me what he will do to me when he comes back and then he leaves. I hear the car.

Mum crawls over. I shrink away from her as she tries to hug me. It hurts too much. Mum gives up, she's asleep and soon snoring.

I crawl away back to my room. It's dark when I come round. I've wet the bed but can't escape the dampness because each move hurts too much. I stare at the ceiling. If Lester wants me to be a good girl tonight then he's out of luck; that thought almost makes me feel better. I'm too smashed up for anything he might want.

Mum comes in. She's brought pills. I swallow some of them, but I worry what they might be because I don't believe she has any normal pills. I drink a little. Not much because the loo is too far for me to crawl. Mum mumbles something about Lester being away for the night. She's on the bed with me. I snuggle up as best as I can do. Her smell of fags is comforting. Mum tried to protect me, didn't she? That's my mum, looking after me, I'll be a good girl, a good snuggly little girl. Then I throw up.

four

There's no way I can work out what will happen next. Lester has no routine. Sometimes he's here, sometimes he's not. He's left me alone for the last few days and I suppose that's because Mum has told him I can't do anything. I heard her shouting at him. Telling him if he wants me to be a good girl it's a bad idea if he almost kills me. Lester just shouted back at her, said he'll find someone else. I could hear Mum getting frantic about that.

Moving still hurts. I can't even make it to the bathroom. Mum has to bring me a bucket and empty it, when she remembers.

Today I will talk to Mouse.

'It's okay,' I say, holding her whiskers to my nose. It's not the same. I put the stuffed toy back under the pillow.

I want Mum to take care of me. Not to bring more pizza and chicken nuggets for every meal. I want to talk to her but most of the time she's so drugged it's her that passes out on my bed. She's so much worse.

'Can't you leave off that stuff for one day?' I plead with her.

'Leave it,' she snaps every time.

'But Mum!'

'Leave it, I said.'

Nothing I can do. I'm not strong enough to start smashing the place up again. Mum's worried. She has only one way to deal with worry and that's to take the drug escape route. I know that because anything real about her disappears and she dissolves into that rag doll floppy state. This time it's bad, she's a mess, looks a mess and even smells a mess. She thinks Lester will chuck us out. She wants me to get better, not for any good reason – just so I can go back to being a good girl.

'Take me away, Mum.'

'I will.'

'When?'

'Leave it.'

Sometimes she says we'll go when we have enough money. That's just the same story. We'll never have enough and even if we do, is Lester going to let us leave with it? Is Lester ever going to let us leave alive? I have nothing else to think of. More days pass. My mattress stinks. Mum and I are wrecked. She still wants to brush my hair.

Lester is going away for a while.

'He's on a job,' Mum tells me more than I expect. She rambles and slurs her words. 'Saw him off with... his work bag,' she laughs and not in a nice way. 'Work bag full of heavy things. Breaking in somewhere, I guess.'

She tells me this and I'm sure I'm meant to be happy, that he's away. I don't get it. I have to call this man Daddy. How does Mum work this out? How can she live with what he does to me? I don't ask her, she might tell me how, she might just tell me she does it for the drugs and she doesn't care what I have to do so long as the stuff keeps coming. So why should she think I'm happy that he's going away? I'm not. Not happy, never am happy, but some of that sick feeling gets a little easier. Maybe that's the best happiness I'll get. It's not very good.

'We have to go,' I say again and again.

Mum says, 'Soon, pet,' more gently and part of me wants that to make me feel better. The rest of me knows it's just wrong.

'Please.'

Mum doesn't answer. Nothing is easier. I have nothing else to fill my head, just Lester. I see him even when he's not there. Every sound in this house is him coming back, coming for me.

I have to make it stop. Mum won't help. There's a glass on the floor, dirty and half-full of water. It still hurts to move but I still reach for it. I want to squeeze until it breaks, make the glass cut into my hand, to make me bleed, will Mum help then? She doesn't even notice; she's staring into nothing.

The glass won't break. I throw it. Against the wall it seems to explode into tiny pieces. Glass pieces cascade into the air. Mum turns her head, and her eyes seem to follow the trickle of water. I see her face and know I've got to her. She snarls and raises her fist. I can see she wants to hit me. There's no mother in here now.

'Go on,' I scream. 'Hit me. That'll stop me being a good girl.'

'Shut it.' Mum raises both fists, but I know she can't do it.

'Hit me and make that man throw us out and no more drugs.'

But she just leaves the room. Above my bed there are books on shelves and pictures fixed to the wall. A few follow the glass before I am too weak to do any more. Throwing things is firmly part of my forever. Mum doesn't come back. I scream but I will not cry. I don't know what will happen next, but for just a moment I have got Lester out of my head. He doesn't leave me for long.

o

Lester has taken the car and we're stuck; he's told us to stay away from the village. Not sure what's out there anyway. It didn't look much of a place when we drove through it. After the first day of no Lester, I hear Mum wandering around the house, opening and closing doors, coming into me and sitting down then jumping up and always going back to look out of the kitchen door. I know what that means. She's worried about where to get her next supplies. She wants Lester to come back. I want him dead. If he doesn't return then Mum will leave, disappear off to find someone who can supply her with the drugs she has to have. I don't know how she would get to them, but I know she would do it somehow. Coming back might be too difficult. I'm always second-best.

I need to recover, at least enough to think about how to get out of here. Mum's promises seem useless. But what can I do? She's told me what the social will do if I'm on my own, and I believe her, 'cos I've heard the same from other kids. Nat said they are all people like Lester. Thinking about Nat is not better, not comforting. She was a bitch, liked seeing how scared we were with her tales of how bad things were going to be for us. I didn't want to believe her but that was hard, because everything she frightened us with was happening to her. Just something else for me not to think about.

But if Mum did take off I can't just stay here and wait for Lester to come back. I must do something. I practise moving. I don't know if anything is broken. I have massive bruises, some from hitting the wall and some from the kicks. They've turned purple and yellow and hurt if I touch them. And hurt even more when I roll over and try to get up. Standing seems impossible so I crawl again. I will do this.

I make it into the kitchen. Not much has been cleared up since I had my throwing fit. Looks like someone just kicked the broken pieces into the corner. I crawl to the bathroom, pull myself up to use the loo, try to wash but give up and just splash a bit of water on my face. I hear Mum upstairs; she doesn't come down so she's probably back in drug zombie time.

I crawl back to the room with my bed. It's exhausting. This room is still Molly-trashed. I try to poke pieces of glass away from my crawling route. The bed doesn't look inviting but I have to lie down, and that's it for the day. I push the covers away, perhaps they will dry out a bit. Not sure because it seems to rain all the time here and the whole house is kind of damp.

Mum brings me some porridge made from a packet she's found. Wish she'd read the instructions. I want her to stay and talk. No, I don't, I'm too afraid of what she might say. Don't tell me the truth.

Next day I crawl some more, pull myself up, try out my legs. Couple of steps before I have to slump down on the floor. I try again. I'm parched and think I should be a bit hungry. I make for the kitchen. I find a dirt-crusted glass and drink some water. It feels better but I am so weak. I must find something to eat. There's nothing I can see except crusts of old pizza. I nibble a bit. The taste of anchovies is still there. I open cupboards and there's nothing, then I find one big cupboard behind a door. Stacks of shelves with ancient packets, flour, sugar, bottles and jars of jam and something labelled "chutney". Everything must be years out of date. I find some tins of beans. Best I can do, there's an ancient tin opener in another drawer. I sit at the table and spoon cold beans into my mouth.

I look at the broken things on the floor. Why did I do it? It just got me wrecked. I don't wish I hadn't done it. I just wish I'd done it better, been stronger. I could have used the poker. Then I think he'd just have taken it from me and hurt me more. He'd have broken bones or something. I want superpowers when all I've got is bruises. I turn back for the bed.

Before I get there, I look ahead, down the corridor to the row of coats and boots. Makes me wonder what happened to the old lady. I bet she was a strong woman, not like me. I stagger on, grab one of the coats and slide down the wall, clutching it to my face, smelling something good. I must have fallen asleep.

Mum shakes me awake. I look at her and for a second I think she is a real mum, not a zombie, and she is behaving in a sort of "normal mum" way too.

'Come on, love.' She hauls me to my feet, and we lurch together back to the kitchen.

Mum's found some more tins and heated something up. Beef stew, it says on the side, next to a best before date which is sometime before I was born. Mum spoons it out onto plates.

'Eat up,' she says, attempting a cheery voice. 'Soon be better.' She says that as though I might have something like measles.

I stare at her. I grip my knife so hard that my arm starts to shake. I will start throwing again. Mum sees it and backs off. Backs right out of the room. The smell of cannabis soon drifts in and mummying is finished. I look at the stew. I tell myself not to lose it. I don't need to plaster the walls with stew,

I need to eat it. 'Breathe, Molly,' I say. I make myself let go of the knife.

I win. Somehow this feels like another victory and I go back to eating. It's not actually that bad. Which is a very good thing because these tins are all there will be until Lester gets back.

What next? I'd dragged the old lady's coat in here with me and it's on the back of my chair. I sniff again, what is it? Not a strong smell, just… well… unusual. Was that what I smelt when I opened the door at the end of my corridor? A nice smell, until I crashed back into the real world.

If I sit here, I am waiting for the only thing that will happen. Lester will come back. He will hit me before and after he says I have to make him happy. He destroys everything, even my time here sitting sniffing an old woman's coat. Every noise is his return. In this room I am right in his way. I may imagine what I can do to make him happy, to somehow make him… make it better, like I want to change my mum. It doesn't happen in forever land although I have not lost all that in my imagination.

Nat told tales for us younger ones to hear, of exactly what the men will do, of how a little powder melted on a spoon will take away your mind and how you will want it to take away the hate.

'Except for hating yourself,' she said, like she was an expert. 'Most of us will kill ourselves,' Nat ends with even more certainty.

I believed she had seen forever too.

I hear a car.

I almost run, don't actually run because it hurts too much, but stumble down past the row of coats after grabbing for my key to the far door, frantic scrabbling with the lock. Lester will catch me. Can I hear him at the other door? In the kitchen? I drop the key. No Lester yet. Poke, poke poke and twist as the lock squeals open, has he heard it? I pull the door, it swings out against creeping ivy. I push into the open. It's quiet. No car, no Lester. I push on outwards.

The air is damp, the ground is wet, and I have no shoes. My shoes are kept for special occasions, good girl times. Oh, and of course someone might have decided it is harder for me to run with no shoes. Hateful shoes with bows and the heel for the child who is an "asset". I like the damp against my feet, well, until I stand on a thistle.

In front of me is a stone wall. A rusting iron gate, grown over by weeds. I'm not stopping now. I grab the iron bars and pull. It opens easily, a well-worn gate even with the weeds and then I'm through.

Whoa.

What? What is this?

I hold tight to the gate and stare.

Wind blows woolly misty clouds across a world of hills and rocks. I have never seen such space. Huge rocks in the distance, over there another enormous hill and there and there. Purple and blue and green. There are no houses. Just hills and rocks and grass. It's so BIG and I am so small. I'm dizzy with the space. Is there nothing in this world that isn't scary?

I need Mouse. I need to show her. I have been horrid leaving her under my pillow and not talking or holding her. As though Mouse is the only thing I can be horrible to, and because of that I am horrible. It is another forever thought.

I turn back towards the house, but I won't have time to get Mouse and I want to look a bit more. The smell on the old lady's coat is out there. I want to walk out, to breathe the air, to walk up the huge hill. Even if I have to crawl, because right now my strength has gone, and it's not gone from Lester's beating. My strength has gone because in front of me is a different forever and I want it. This different forever smells so good, even if it is a bit damp.

I look again. What is that? It's a woolly monster. A four-legged woolly beast. There's another. They aren't really scary, they're kind of cute. Eating the grass. They don't look like cows or sheep. Is this all magic?

I must get back. I must get inside before I'm missed. If they know I've seen this then they'll take it away. I will never see this place again. I am more scared than before. I have started to think. The other girls told me over and over, you must turn off your mind, then no disappointments. Don't hope, there is none. Wipe it from your mind.

I can't do it. Tears tumble down my face. I slip inside, locking the door behind me. Maybe this time I have got away with it. There's no shouting yet. I have seen something so beautiful. If they take that away that will hurt more than any beating.

I make it to the kitchen. Mum and Lester sit sharing out different coloured pills between them. They don't speak to me, what they're doing is more important. Lester swallows a handful of blue ones. I hope my face doesn't show what I have seen. I shuffle to the kettle, make them tea in the hope they won't ask. I can barely stand; the pain has returned. I hold on to the sink. Is that Lester calling me over? No idea. The floor is rising to meet me.

I don't think I am out of it for long. In a blurred haze I see Mum with Lester on the mattress. She's doing her best to be the good girl. Lester is slurring that he wants the real one. Mum sees me stir and shoots the hardest of looks. I'm to stay down. Mum is doing her best. I suddenly realise that she was once me. Of course, I should have known. She has reached forever. It's a family business.

five

I could have ended up with Grandma. Would that have been better?

There was a time before we moved to London. A blurry time. Is it just being young, when you arrive somewhere, and the past seems to vanish? I know when I was much younger things were never exactly normal.

Gran and Mum seemed both to have the same miserable feelings about everything. Everything was wrong, everyone else was to blame. But they could never agree. They had to argue all the time. If they were alone the shouting would soon start, shouting and breaking things and throwing things.

Gran had something wrong with her chest. I guess it was years of smoking.

'If I wasn't so ill, I'd get out and make real money,' Gran would say before she spat into a bucket she always had near her.

That led to Mum saying, 'You've never made any money.'

It was like a firework being lit, words exploding between them, worse if something breakable was nearby.

But even those arguments seem blurred. It might have been Mum telling me about them, were they real? Did Gran really spend her time coughing and spitting? It is easy to picture it, Gran and her bucket of spit, yuck. Could have just been Mum wanting me to believe it. Mum doesn't feel the need to stick to the truth about anything.

I don't know much about Gran, or Mum really. It was Gran's house in a long row of the same houses. It wasn't very clean, either in the house or outside. No one had much money, or any money at all.

Neither of them could look after me. That's what Dor said. Doreen was Gran's sister, probably, and slightly less chaotic. I lived with her. Everyone called her Dor. Took me ages to work that out, especially since anytime Mum came round it wasn't long before I was told to 'shut it'. But she didn't come often.

Dor was ordinary. I don't think she took drugs. She didn't have men coming at odd times. She didn't hit me much, smacks when I was naughty. But naughty meant talking back or not doing what I was told, not smashing every breakable thing in the room, not like now.

I don't know how long she looked after me. Mum tells me stuff and it's even harder to know whether to believe what she tells me about Dor. I guess I just accepted it, living with Dor. I was told Gran and Mum were too sick for me to live with them. That didn't make sense, but so many things were like that.

For a while I went to school with other children. I sort of remember playing in a school yard, running about, shrieking and chasing. Real school. Amazing to think that I went to school, talked to other kids, maybe had friends, came back to Dor's house, ate tea, went to bed. It all worked, and I thought it was normal. I had a few toys and stuff, no Mouse then, but I had a doll called Emily – she was posh. At least I thought she was posh, in a lime green frock and loads of hair. Dor really didn't have much money, but I was used to putting up with things. Just not a lot of cuddling. Not a lot of food, either. Now I wonder if Mum paid Dor.

One day I came home. I had a key by then. Still not quite sure how old I was, it didn't seem to matter which class I was in. The school was just along the road and I could come down the street on my own. I didn't think a lot about Lester types being around, although we heard about them.

On that day, the house seemed quiet. Usually, Dor was in the kitchen making tea for us. This time she was in the kitchen but not doing anything normal. No use trying to stop myself thinking about this, it has glued itself into my brain. I can bring that picture up in my head anytime. Doreen is stretched out on the floor with her clothes all in a mess, her head is twisted, dribble coming out of her mouth and she's mumbling and twitching her arm as though she's trying to get up.

I ran back out into the street and started screaming and screaming. I don't remember much after that and I never saw Dor again. I don't know how to miss her. In the end I was told she'd had a stroke, but I didn't know what that was. By the time they told me about the stroke I didn't ask questions and certainly got no answers. I was living back with Mum, and Gran.

Strange place, Gran's, even without the shouting. There were lots of things you couldn't talk about, parts of life just missing.

No sign of a grandfather, no mention of him. No photos around the house of anyone in a family type of way. Actually, no photos at all. Gran hadn't always been there; she'd been somewhere else. When I was in London, Nat told me my gran had been in prison. Might be true, might not.

I did ask about my dad. Mostly I asked at the wrong time, that being any time really. Mum would get cross and say she didn't want to talk about it (Dad being an it). 'Occupational hazard,' she called him, not a useable sort of name. At the time I suppose I didn't know about sex, didn't understand what an occupational hazard could be although Mum seemed to have lots of them.

And it went wrong pretty quickly, or I was told I went wrong. When Gran and Mum weren't shouting at each other they were shouting at me. Nothing I ever did was right. Smacking happened a lot. There were men. That's when I found out what Mum did for a job, did it in the back bedroom. I just didn't know, then, what "it" was exactly. No one put it into words I could understand.

Nothing was normal anymore. School fell apart. I remember feeling so angry and not knowing why. I got into fights, lost most of them, got smacked for having a bloody nose, got smacked for giving someone a bloody nose. I was supposed to have done something bad and hurt one of the boys. Useless to say it wasn't me. All sorts of people came to the school, came to our house. Police. Lots more shouting.

Maybe I was too young to remember or maybe I was old enough to forget. Anyway the social had found us. For a short while I was taken to something called a foster home. A house, white-painted, I remember that. A family, Mum and Dad and two boys. It didn't last. At that house I did break more things. They put me back with Mum, but we weren't left alone.

People came to ask me questions. People: some nice, some bored, some stroppy and some in a hurry. Quite a lot in a hurry. No idea what they were talking about, made Mum and Gran more on edge. That meant more shouting.

There wasn't much in the house. Sometimes I was sent out to get something to eat – from the chip shop. The people in a hurry always asked what we were eating. I think they actually wanted to know about other things but seemed afraid to ask. I suppose Gran and her bucket frightened them a bit. I was always told to keep quiet and I didn't tell them about the drugs, the booze or the men. I had a feeling they had already guessed about those things.

One day I woke up and our bags had been packed. Well, one bag was all we had. And we were off, dragged off. Gran didn't say anything, not even goodbye, just spat into her bucket and said it was about time we left. Mum said we had to get out before the social got both of us. She told me that they would put us in prison unless we got away. That made me scared.

I remember I wasn't very well, tummy aches and being sick. We kept on moving from place to place, room to room in houses with more shouting but no Gran. I don't know if she is still alive. If I ask Mum, she just shrugs and doesn't answer.

I suppose there must have been people looking for us. Perhaps they still are. Perhaps they've got better things to do. I'm starting to hope they will find me; prison doesn't sound so bad. Can they find me before Lester uses his poker? Because what Lester hasn't said, but is quite obvious to me, is that after he's smashed Mum, he's going to turn on me.

six

It's harder now, I can't stop thinking about the world outside the back door, so huge, so amazing, I must see it again. NO, Molly. Turn it off. Blank out that space, those hills, the smell of grass. Blank out what you saw in those seconds: the specks of purple and yellow so far out into a distance of emptiness. Forget the great tumbled down piles of black rock lined up against the sky. You can't have any of that because there is something much larger out there, something I could see while I held tight to the gate, thinking my legs would give way. The thought that comes back to me over and over again as I lie on the old lady's bed, because what is out there is hope. And hope really scares me.

Nat just went on about hope. The thing that will always fail you.

'Once you start to hope you will always lose out. Don't EVER start to hope,' she said.

That made sense to all of us. We all saw hope on the telly, worlds of people and their problems. We were experts in disappointment, like hoping Mum would come back one day without the drugs; it was never going to happen. Hoping that perhaps something would change – for the better – when all it did was change for the worse. So I really don't need hope right now. Good girls don't need hope; with it I am so much easier to hurt and Lester does like to hurt me.

o

I have to snatch times outside. Mouse comes out on the moor with me now. We've agreed not to talk about hope. We just look out at things and Mouse looks with me.

'What do you think of this place?' I ask her and hold her up to my ear.

'Absolutely,' I say, because I always agree with Mouse now. We don't mention the difficult stuff.

But it had to happen. Lester was always going to find me outside the back door. Had to happen because I can't resist. Often in the middle of the night I'd sneak out into the moonlight. I don't go far. I just stand and stare. There are no other lights out here, no streetlamps, no streets and the moon shines so brightly. In that light what is out there seems even larger and so empty. Occasionally I hear a sound; it just has to be an owl, they really do hoot. I can almost feel the sound.

My night-time visits turn to daytime sneaking out. A small noise makes me turn from the gate back to the house. He's standing there. Something on his face is different. I don't understand. I know when he wants to hit me, I know when he wants to do worse, but this? What is it? Lester seems to stare straight through me, then he turns and almost runs the few steps back to the house. I hear a sound. Lester makes a sound like a baby. A whimper. I follow slowly. I have another dangerous thought because as well as hope I have now seen fear on Lester's face. There is something out here on the moor that frightens him. And I like that.

Of course, he hits me. 'What you doing out there? Told you not to go out there.' He hadn't told me, and he can't speak without shaking. 'Never go out there again.' He sounds frantic.

I don't like the slapping I get, and it is a slapping, and I don't understand. I want to work out what it could be that frightens him. Can I find out? Could I find the thing that frightens him and use it?

Nat is back in my head telling me not to be stupid – 'it's just another hope, put it away, won't happen, can't happen, blank out the slaps and pain.' But I can't. Whatever it was has changed something, he stops hitting me. He's unsure, turns away.

'Don't let her out there again on the moor.' His voice cracks as he says the words to Mum.

So that's what it's called. The moor.

I see Mum register it. She's an expert in seeing weakness. I guess she knows it will not last. That Lester will soon become himself again. Now he still looks scared.

Mum uses it, I'm sure she wants to get something from him while there is a chance. First, as always, for the money she needs to buy her supplies – Lester hands it over. Then, chancing her luck. 'Oh, Molly won't come to no harm out there, no one around, keep her healthy, you can always call her back.'

Lester opens his mouth, but words don't come. I can see sweat on his face. I back away.

Mum pushes on, 'Won't do any harm. She knows what will happen if she causes trouble.' Mum shoots me a glance; her face is blank. Is she telling me what will happen, or has Lester told her about the poker and the broken legs he's planned?

'Fine,' Lester croaks and stamps off to the garage.

Mum and I look at each other. She shrugs. I want to ask her questions. She says, 'Leave it,' like she does about so much. I can see she has an idea and doesn't want to share it with me. I want to know. She walks away with me shouting after her. I feel it's like some sort of treasure and Mum is going to keep it. What makes Lester scared is her protection; I'm the one who really needs it.

'Nothing is fair for us.' More of Nat's words creep into my head.

Mum will do anything for drugs. Fairness isn't in it.

I don't think about Lester for long. I never want to waste time thinking about that man. I do think about Mum. I saw her face. Now she thinks she's got him we're not leaving here. She thinks she can win, turn Lester to get her way. She won't. Mum always loses. I always lose with her.

But I am allowed to go out, because Lester doesn't want to talk about what there is outside. Days later he sets up the whistle routine. Or was it Mum? I get it, I have to run back when I hear it, or before if I can. Why does he have to go over it more than once? He shows me where he'll stand, makes me hear the noise, almost frantic to make sure I understand.

He'll stand by the back door. 'Just inside,' he says and pulls me down the corridor. 'Right here.' As though that is the most important thing in the world.

'If you make me come out and get you, then…' He stops. I'm waiting to hear how he'll break legs and other bones, but he doesn't go on. There is something out there which he can't deal with. It doesn't make him a better man, just a weaker man. He'll soon get back his violence and his needs.

'What is it?' I ask Mouse, but she doesn't reply.

o

And of course, it fills all my thoughts. I can see how this place called the moor is scary for me. But not in a Lester sort of way. At first, I'd stayed so near to the gate, not daring to go out into that wild place. What does it do to Lester? Mum won't explain and I'm not sure she really knows. I need to find out, to find something to protect myself – no one else is going to do that. If it's bad for Lester it has to be good for me. Too late to go out there now. Tomorrow?

There is no need for me that night. Tonight, there is a new balance. Mum wanders the house, occasionally humming. It's not a good noise. Lester turns to his drink. Not long before he passes out, even too drunk to hit anyone tonight. In the morning he's angry.

I hope there's something in his head still frightening him but Mum says it's the job he's meant to be doing. Something that's going to take him away for a few more days. The way she whispers it tells me it's definitely nothing legal.

Mum runs Lester down to meet some man after he's checked through a bag of tools, again. She says later that Lester is scared of the man, who owns a proper garage with cars needing repairs. So that's two things scaring Lester, this gets better. She still gives me no explanation.

Mum says Lester is just a bully as though he isn't that important. I know he's a bully because I'm the one getting bullied. Her saying that makes no difference to me.

With Lester away, Mum goes shopping. Shopping with Lester's money. She says that while she's got the money she's not going to go into town at night. I thought we were saving so that we could leave. Mum says there will be enough when

Lester gets back from whatever he's doing.

Mum doesn't take me shopping.

'In case anyone sees you and starts asking questions.'

'Wouldn't that be good?' I ask.

'You want me to go to jail,' she snaps. 'Then they'd put you somewhere forever.'

I never win arguments. Getting put away forever seems likely whatever I do. But it does make me think that someone might be looking for us, for me.

o

Out on the moor my forever seems so different. It does not match. This fantastic outside, so beautiful it fills my eyes with tears much more easily than anything Lester does. The moor and the house, places so different it has to be another universe. Lester and Mum live in a different place, they don't see the moor, they can't see that everything real is out here, not in the foul violent drug-fuelled mess that they make, that they will make mine as well. I can't change them, but I can bring a bit of the moor feeling back. I will tidy.

I have the crazy idea that making this place more of a home will make a difference. With Mum on a drug run and Lester doing whatever he does at the garage, I will tidy.

I start in the kitchen, the hardest room, Lester's room. It hurts to be in there. Can I do this? I give up and go back to look outside. It doesn't make me stronger or think that this is actually going to make any difference, but I return to the kitchen.

My room and the corridor to the moor look like add-ons to this house. Different building, I think it must be newer.

As well as the walking stuff there is a cupboard with cleaning things: a broom, a mop and bucket, old brushes, a shovel – no Hoover.

I take the broom to the kitchen. There is still a mound of broken plates and the things I threw. I sweep, pushing the broom hard. I want to clean Lester out of this room. Soon I have a pile of all the rubbish of his life, the broken stuff mixed with empty bottles, empty fag packets and in the sink a mountain of dirty glasses and mugs and the few unbroken plates.

There are bottles of something that looks like washing-up liquid in the store cupboard, it is my secret cave of magic and a strange mix of things someone might have bought because they were on a cheap offer.

I wash, scrub the sink clean, clean the grease from the window. I think of getting out and clearing the bushes, one day; I will make them see outside – I give a gurgled laugh, Lester won't like it.

Lester.

He's not back but he is always in this room. Over there, in the corner, on his mattress. Where the worst things happen. I have been pushing everything away from it. Keeping my back to his space. The smell, the dirty mess, it is all Lester. It will take more than a broom to tackle that. I know there is an ancient washing machine in the bathroom, and a cupboard with some unused linen. No, Molly. You will fall too low.

I go back to my swept pile. I find some plastic bags and shovel the stuff into them. I chuck the bags down the end of the hall. I'm not going out on the other side of the house. Lester will appear. I am nowhere near brave enough to go looking for him.

All this time, Mouse has been sitting on the kitchen table.

I hear her words. Not all of them are nice. The room is cleaner, but the smell is still here. I try to open a window; it is jammed shut and no matter how hard I push, it will not open. I risk opening the door with the broken pane of glass. The wind screams in, it is fantastic, even Lester's side of the house cannot get rid of the moor.

I hear the car.

Shutting the door, I run back to my room. Mum and Lester are together. I wait. I want to hear them gasp at the clean, tidy place I have made. I sneak back to peer through the door opening. I must be careful; sneaking comes before pain. But I want to see Mum smile at how I have made this a little of the nice place she had promised.

Nothing.

They are sharing out pills and packets. They have not noticed the room. Mouse told me they wouldn't, that they didn't care what was around them because their world wasn't here, it was in some faraway stare. I didn't want to believe Mouse.

With a sick feeling I edge forward into the room.

'What do you want?' Lester curls his lip.

'Mol.' Mum nearly makes a smile.

I point around the room.

'What?' Mum's smile drops.

'I… I… cleaned it up,' I say with something sounding even younger than my supposed nine years.

'Nice,' Mum says as she tries to snatch back some of Lester's stash.

'Thieving cow.' Lester grabs them back.

They are into a full-grown drug row. It is no use. I am no use. I stumble away.

'Do my room next time,' Mum laughs at my back.

'And my fucking mattress.' Lester knows exactly what he says.

My head is buried into the bedclothes. But I am dry-eyed. I will not break. I will have my moor. I will, I will, I will.

'Get in here,' I hear his shout later.

seven

Before my throwing attack, things on the shelf above the bed were neatly arranged. I've started putting them back in place. It's not my room but I feel badly for the old woman.

After my tidying session in the kitchen, I've found it hard to stop. No one seems to want me today and I set about this room. First the broken things, sweeping and shovelling the mess into more plastic bags. I use up the ones that came with the pizzas, but I search the broom cupboard and take the bucket. Lester is away, Molly just has to get braver – or so Mouse says, since she's changed from telling me just bad things – so we go out of the door to the garage and I find a dustbin. There's nothing in it. Was whatever happened to the old lady after a bin day? Is that why the bin is empty?

Bin day? I don't think there is one, never heard any lorries coming up here. Maybe you have to take the rubbish down to the village. I don't have any idea. I just shove my swept-up bucketful into the bin. The broken glass makes a clang. Mouse shouts, 'BOO.' And I jump, but it's still quiet.

I decide to look around a bit further. The kitchen door isn't the front door to this house. That must be behind the curtain in the hall. From outside I see the front of the house with steps leading up to it. They are covered in weeds, but this really must have been a grand place at some time.

Back inside, I'm thinking I haven't got long. Lester and Mum won't care what I do, but they come and take a look if they hear any noise. I want to finish clearing up in this room without them noticing. Part of that is because I want to see if there is anything else hidden in this room – like a gun perhaps, but not likely.

Apart from the tin of keys there is nothing else hidden under the mattress, and there's not much else in the room. Nothing that looks useful, just clothes and junk.

Strange, that whoever lived here has been totally removed from the rest of the house, everywhere except this room. Even that has been ransacked. Or has it? If I look around it seems as though not everything has been touched. There's a drawer of clothes, still folded. Lester comes into this room. Sometimes he pretends to be nice; it doesn't always end that way. When he does come in here, he looks around as though he's lost something.

I find myself thinking about whoever lived here, more and more, wondering if she might be like my gran, or maybe nicer. I invent her. A nice old lady who cares about people. The few of her old bits left in this room feel good except when I think she may be buried in the garden. Mouse often tells me about the patch of ground which has been dug up; I don't look at it.

o

On one of the shelves, I find a map. It's an old bashed-up over-used sort of map. One belonging to the old lady, whoever she was, I suppose.

I don't understand maps. This one has lots of brown and green and it just has to be a map of the moor – Dartmoor, it says on the outside. The brown bits have strange names like Hangingstone Hill, Hound Dog Tor and Cosdon Beacon. Could be anything. Someone has drawn lines on it with numbers. They all run back to one place. Could that be where we are?

They are back. It's chicken nugget time. Then it's drug and alcohol time. Lester is out of it. Mum made sure of that and she uses the time to remove cash from his wallet. It's a dangerous thing to do and I run back to my room. I am starting to like my room and that's dangerous too.

Nat would have told me not to do the tidying. 'If you've got anything nice, someone else will take it; mess is best for girls like us.'

But I can't do it. The moor has changed me, and by the light of another bare bulb, I study the map.

The next day I take it out with me. Whatever Lester is planning, it is taking him away from here.

I'm braver and walk away from the house, up the hill to an iron pole. What's that for? Somebody's iron pole. There's no one about. Sometimes I see people walking out on the moor. Groups of dog walking people, a few with heavy rucksacks on their backs. I want to run up to them, ask for help, but then Lester will smash up my mum and it will all be my fault. I have to save her. Just make sure I don't fill my mind with what you have to do before any saving might happen.

'Hello.'

I jump a mile up the iron pole.

'It's a flagpole,' says the lady who has appeared from nowhere. I should run, but I don't. I stare at her, taking in her wild look, hair swept all over the place, a friendly face but slightly squiffy, as though one side has moved the wrong way.

'They put a flag on it when they are shooting.' She puts her hand to her face, covering the side I'm staring at.

'Shooting?' I say the word but most of it is in my head. Shooting sounds likely. Lester probably has men with guns on patrol out here. Looking for good girls on the run. Good job I found that out. Might have run off, got shot at and dragged back to see what he'd done with the poker. I turn away from the woman, ready to disappear back down the hill.

'Wait,' she says, and it sounds a bit frantic.

I don't want to stay out here now with this crazy woman. She's dressed in the same sort of coat that hung in the old woman's house, green and loads of pockets. I should have put one on. Now it's getting cold and I'm wearing the wrong clothes, unless I have to… does this woman… surely… I look into her eyes for a second and all I see are questions. I'm off.

I pull away from her, noticing for the first time that she was holding me by the arm. I'm sprinting down the hill. She's calling me back. I don't stop. Maybe she's safer than Lester but maybe not. I hide in some bushes, prickly bushes, but I don't want that woman to see where I'm going because I've dropped the map and I really don't want her bringing it back to Lester's house. She mustn't know where we are living. I wait, and the woman seems to just disappear.

Slowly I make my way back down to the house, even though there's not been a whistle. No woman, no map, no hope. But no Lester. Doesn't matter, the house is still full of him, every sound and I jump. I have recovered from the worst beating but it didn't leave just bruises. Inside the house I am a hollow person. I'm back inside, in my room.

I've just realised. If Lester notices that I've done the tidying, then he may demand that I do his bed. I can't and I am sick with the thought. It makes me retch, it is a noise, Mum comes into the room.

'Better,' she says, and she does notice what I have done. She turns to leave.

'Mum…?' I start.

She gives me a snarl, 'What?' I know she's expecting questions.

'Can you…?'

'What now?' she snaps.

'Can you…?'

'WHAT?' she shrieks. Lucky that Lester is still out, or he would have come in.

'Make his bed, I can't do it,' I say too quietly and have to repeat it.

Mum shakes her head as though I have asked for the moon.

I show her the cupboard with the linen. There is a lot of moaning and puffing but she does it. I don't watch. I blot it out. I hum to myself with my fingers in my ears. It makes no difference. Nothing can take away what Lester has done to me. What he does, what he does THERE, in that stinking corner. Mum shuffles off. I cry. The word – humiliation – doesn't do what I feel. Shame is nearer. I am a thing, not a person and I am all the words of shame.

o

The next day I am too scared to go out on the moor again. It nags at me. I want it. I want to be out there again. I suppose I want to see that woman again. I shouldn't, but the pull is too strong. Next day, still no Lester. I take a coat; Mouse is in one of the pockets. She's asking me not to go, I don't answer.

I take another route to the flagpole. There's no flag. I don't know what that means but didn't that woman say they put a flag up the pole when there was shooting? So did no flag mean I was safe? Made me think we should have a flag at the house for when Lester was there. No safety with him about. Give me a gun, please.

'Hello again.'

More jumping. Where does she come from? I'd had my head full of the sort of stuff I didn't want inside of me. She'd crept up on me while I fought to get rid of them. That meant I'm not safe. I make to run, but again she has hold of my arm, tighter this time. I could still get away, but something holds me back; actually, it is the map.

'You dropped it.' She tries a smile, and it makes her face look worse. Again, she moves her hand up to hide it.

'Know what it is?' She sits down on the grass, opening up the map in front of her. She's let go of me and I step away, step back, away. She pats the ground next to her. Wanting me to sit and I want to sit but I'm scared, cold scared, despite my now wearing one of the old lady's coats over my good girl uniform. I crouch, ready to run.

The map flaps in the breeze and she folds it to a smaller shape. 'That's where we are.' She points at a mass of squiggly brown lines. 'That's Belstone Tor.' She raises her hand and points at the nearest pile of rocks. 'That's it, up there.'

I'd looked at them before. Belstone Tor wasn't the name I'd given it. The rocks were old man, big dog and mushroom to me. She points out the names of other hills. The map is making sense. I have moved from crouch to my knees and then sitting as she talks. I don't mind her face. I want to curl up next to her while she talks about the places. I want to know their real names, it makes them real, makes this place real for me.

The whistle goes.

I grab the map, leap up and charge down the hill. I hear her voice calling. I have to get away.

Lester is near berserk. He's at the back door. Poker in hand.

'I was just going to use it,' he tries to snarl at me, but behind me is the moor and whatever it does to him it makes his snarl more of a whimper. Have I made him whimper? I stop. But that makes him worse, red-faced, his whole body going rigid, and he turns away. I know what he's going to do.

'Stop, stop.' I run to him, grab his arm, struggle weakly to stop him from going into the kitchen. I can hear Mum in there. I imagine Lester breaking her legs. 'Stop. I'll be a good girl. I'll do anything you want. Please stop.'

Lester turns and knocks me to the ground. 'Of course you will.' He's back to strength, normal Lester, which is not normal at all. He doesn't break Mum's legs. I see Mum going out of the kitchen as he drags me in. He doesn't break my legs either. But afterwards I do cry. Silently the tears stream down my face. I am much weaker now. My world has maps and tors and the woman. It can be hurt more easily now I've done all the things Nat told me not to do.

Lester laughs at my tears. He likes my tears. I think he likes to hurt me more than the other things he does. Those things don't seem to make him happy at all, just meaner. I leave the room. He doesn't call me back.

eight

We have two sorts of days – Lester days and no-Lester days. Neither day is good. When he isn't there, I forget. I talk to Mouse in the sort of way I used to do, we talk about the weather when it's too bad to go outside, we talk about the state of the bathroom, we plan our next walk with the map and wonder if that woman will be outside. Mouse runs over the bed, sniffs at the sheets, ignores the stains. I become Molly.

A floorboard creak, a banging door, a car in the distance, anything and I am not Molly in that instant. I stop, rigid, listening. I hold my breath. As though if I stop, it will stop. It doesn't. If he appears, I wait and hope. If he doesn't appear, I wait and hope. It is never up to me what happens. I drop things, break things without throwing them. I do not know what to do. I have stopped tidying.

Actually, it was Mum who told me to stop doing things in the house. I'm not entirely clear that I understand. She muttered something about being too old. It took me a while, but I think she meant that nine-year-old Molly wouldn't do these things. It meant I looked a bit older, not such the good girl that Lester would want. Tidying means older. Good and bad. What will Lester do? I stop tidying because... I don't know why I stop.

Mum seems to have got enough stuff to keep her away from the world, only drug days for her. I try again to talk, say she should stop. Sometimes she weeps and tries to hug me and says she will, but only tomorrow or some other time or day or year that is not today. I tell her I want to leave, and she says we will, and it has the same time scale. I know that is never until the money and the drugs run out. Lester is loaded after his last job, but I guess they are both going quickly through the cash; will Mum be storing any away?

Lester talks about a holiday. 'Something by the sea,' he slurs one night. I've been told to just stand there in case. If it's going to happen, I want to get it over. I'm hoping he'll forget me, not hit me too hard, not kick me. It's a sick feeling inside of me when every move he makes could be the way it starts again. No point in hoping about any other stuff, that's not going to happen. We are not going on holiday. Lester realises that pretty quickly. I see his mind cloud over. I could have helped speed it up.

'No, Mr Lester, a holiday is a bad idea because someone might hear the screams and see the bruises after one of my good girl nights.' That's what I would have said. 'Also, my mum can barely stand with all the stuff you've been giving her. She can't make sandcastles or take me on donkey rides or paddle – she'd drown in shallow water.' We don't go on holiday. Lester's boss has told him about another job. The boss is not some high-powered manager or a normal executive of a respectable firm. Whatever they plan it will take him away for a while.

Good when Lester is away. Worse when he comes back. Much worse when I don't know which it will be. I know this will come to an end. It will end badly like all the other places I've been with Mum. So it might be better if Lester stayed because the end will come more quickly. I can't completely stop hoping, that is what the moor has done for me. I think it is the hope that stops me from going berserk again, but I am wrong. I don't smash the place up again because I am too afraid. I don't tidy either.

This will end badly. Really, I know it will end with the poker. Lester will kill us. We cannot leave. Mouse tells me that in the dark. She tells me to run, not to worry about Mum and the poker. I could run, in the old lady's boots, I could run. But I think there is only one road out of here. Lester would follow me, bring me back, make me watch.

I don't run. Later, when I am Molly, I take out the map, remember the names the woman told me. Who is she? I don't think about her for long because the map is really interesting now it makes sense. The lines and numbers look like they show how far it is to places from where I am. How far to Steeperton, Yes Tor, and other hills. It's miles to some of the places, did the woman who lived here walk all that way? I wonder if she is in hospital. I'm not going to look at that patch in the garden that looks to have been dug recently. It is just another very scary idea that I have. If she didn't get out of here alive, what chance do we have? I look at the map again.

I can't take my eyes off this huge paper picture of the moor. I don't need to hide it. Lester searches my room, pretty much chucks everything around. Don't know what he expects me to have hidden because I have nothing. I'd like to have all sorts of dangerous things – guns, bombs – but I don't. But the map I just put back on the shelf. Lester doesn't look at the old lady's things, so it's hidden from him. When Mouse isn't with me she hides in a drawer with the old lady's underwear. I worry about Mouse, she is so much a part of me.

As days go by, I'm getting left alone more, I guess Lester is getting bored with me, perhaps even stopping tidying hasn't worked. I feel a little older. The moor makes me older than tidying. There are many confusions and things in my head that I hate. There seems only one person in this world who wants me, and he is a sick violent pervert.

Nat said it would be like that. 'Only perves will want you.'

When she said that I didn't have the full picture. I didn't understand what she meant when Nat added, 'And it'll be you that wants them back because there is no one else.'

In the dark lonely times, I think and hate and worry and hate mostly the thoughts that come into my head when I don't want them. What is going to happen next? Being left alone means I can at least slide out onto the moor.

o

I go out and look for the woman. She's not there, not by the flagpole and not up on the hill. The one that's called Belstone Tor on the map, my map. I walk on. I'm going uphill and soon I'm short of breath. I'm not used to this exercise and moving is still painful, but I will go on, come on Molly, and I mutter with a left step 'kill' and right step 'him'. My voice rises and my hopes of murder are nearly shouted as I reach the top, left KILL, right HIM.

Panting, I lean against some stones, and panting I look around. If I look in front of me there are no houses, no signs of anything manmade except an ancient stone wall running down towards a stream in the valley.

I check out what I can see with the names on the map. The wall has a name – Irishman's wall – weird because I'm sure we are a long way from Ireland. A way over the valley there's a huge dome of a hill. It's all colours, so many shades of green with dots of white sheep all over. I'm not breathing. I am so small in this place, so small and I want it to swallow me up because it is so beautiful. For one second it is just me and the moor, wind on my face, blows away anything else.

A sound, a shout, a gasp of breath. There are some people out here, walking. A group of four, older people, talking. They are miles away, but their voices echo across at me. There are no children, I suppose they are all at school. If someone spotted me, on my own, then it would be like London again and whoever the social are they'd be after me. Can't happen. If it did then Lester is going to take it out on Mum. Smashing her up with the poker really will happen. Probably will happen anyway but I mustn't let it be my fault. The woman I met didn't ask me about school, odd that.

I turn for Lester's home, it's a trudge now downhill, clouds cover the sky. A fine drizzle. Less beautiful now and the huge open space could be a bit scary, unless you think what is ahead of you and start to hope for lightning and a quick end. Tears again in my eyes. I run to keep my map dry.

A no-Lester day. No Lester the next day either.

o

When I go out again, I pick out a coat with a hood, and I've found some old trousers that must have belonged to whoever it really was that lived here, or maybe still does if she's just ill. The clothes are made for someone small, fit me quite well and from a distance you'd think I was just some old walker. Lots of the walkers look just the same.

This time I go over the first hill to see what the next one looks like: Oke Tor. As I hike up the hill the smell of the moor is all around. There's plenty of mud to avoid but between the soggy patches there are purple and yellow flowers and often birds shoot out when I get near. I run after them. Once I found myself laughing at them in a silly way. Mouse tells me I am being a child. I don't want this to stop. I don't understand how being out here makes you feel... I'm just talking to myself in my head and I have to stop because I nearly said this place makes you feel free.

'You'll never be free,' Nat had said. 'When you get older, they stuff you full of drugs and that's your life.' I realise that Mouse is becoming a shadow of Nat. It's really Nat who is saying these things now. I have brought Nat with me.

But I am free out here with the wind again in my face, great mountains of cloud blowing over the sky and always the emptiness of Dartmoor, the name on the map. Dartmoor and it's beautiful. Until it rains. Which it does often. Sometimes the wind just screams at you and hurls water in bucketfuls. Then even in this coat, which looks like it's made for walking out here, even with that on you get soaked. I guess that's why she had several coats, to let one dry. She must have done a lot of walking. I try to imagine her, walking here, in the rain. I hope she loved it. I must try again looking through things in the house to see if there is anything that will tell me something about her. I walk faster to drive the house out of my head.

I reach the top of Oke. I stop. It's taken me a while to get here. Most of the worst bruises are healed but I will get new ones when Lester comes back. Now I'm thirsty and a bit hungry. I should have brought something. There are pools of water. I don't fancy drinking from them, they are too dark and muddy. Down in the valley there's a stream. But I want to go on a bit more along the top of this ridge. I'm sort of imagining the lumps of rock dotted everywhere are people. People to talk to. They may not talk back but they don't hit you.

I've stopped again. Mouse and I are in mid-conversation with a huge stone that looks like a dog's head. I hear a noise, it's a whistle. Not Lester's hateful noise, something different. I sink down behind the dog rock. Hope it doesn't bark.

'Shh,' I say to Mouse.

I can't see who made the whistle. From where I am hiding, I can see down to a small bridge. I keep very still. Something strange is happening and I can't work out what it is. A way off, I see a bush move, then another. I rub my eyes. One of the bushes is moving fast, almost tumbling down towards the bridge and it stands up; it's not a bush, it's someone dressed in camouflage. More bushes are on the run towards the bridge. Suddenly two soldiers step out, soldiers with guns pointing. I freeze; are they going to be killed? Everyone stops, looking at each other. The bushy person turns and blows the whistle again. All the other bushes stand up and walk down to join the first. No shooting yet. Someone laughs. Then the whole lot break out and sit on the ground opening their packs. I watch and they're having lunch. What is this?

I can't resist. I crawl down towards them. Slowly. They don't see me. My tummy rumbles. I crawl on between other, real, small bushes. One of the soldiers has left their pack at the edge of the group and gone off for a pee. Sandwiches. I can see them, just a few feet away. I inch closer, stretch out for food.

'Oi.'

Hands grab me from behind. I'm hauled to my feet, shaking. Maybe they will shoot me. The soldiers gather round. They shout words which make no sense. I look around. They are all soldiers. They are all black. They are all women. Except one.

'What are you doing?' says the only man soldier and, as it turns out, the only person from this country.

I say nothing. One of the other soldiers still grips me by the arm.

'Speak up,' the man says, more loudly than before.

What should I say? Tell them about Lester, about Mum? They could all march up there and set us free. Even if they got in before Lester smashed her up she wouldn't want rescuing, she wasn't being held captive, she had put us there in the first place. I loved Mum as much as I hated her. There wasn't anyone else. No other family you'd want, no friends that were any better off than me. The trouble was that all these thoughts shot through my brain while they waited for me to answer the man's questions. And these last few days on the moor have shown me another world, one I can't have; I am so much weaker now. I hang my head and the tears dribble down my face.

I guess the man thought I was older. He leans forward and shakes me. 'Come on, you were doing a bit of thieving? Eh?'

He is going to shake me again, probably a slap or two are in his mind. Seems to be a common event for me, I seem to attract this. But one of the other women puts an arm on his shoulder. The other women soldiers close in.

'What?' The man turns to them. 'You all gone soft? You're here for training. This girl's a thief. She needs a good lesson.'

'Non,' one of them says and puts her arm around me.

The male soldier shrugs his shoulders. And somehow, we

all end up sitting on the ground with me eating their lunch. The man wasn't going to join in, but the women kept on in their own language and eventually he gave in and sat next to me and actually said sorry.

'Not a great idea to sneak up to armed soldiers and try to pinch their lunch,' he tells me, almost with a smile.

I nod with my mouth full. This was real food, even if it was their packed lunch.

'Didn't you bring anything with you?'

'Left it all behind,' I mutter in the end as the best thing I could think of saying. True really, I had left everything behind somewhere.

'She speaks!' The man laughs, and the others join in.

He explains they are a group of soldiers from some place in Africa who have come over here for training on Dartmoor.

'We're all based up at the army camp.' He waves his arm, suggesting the camp was somewhere over one of the big hills. 'Do a lot of training out here on Dartmoor.'

He tells me they only speak French and he is the translator and I look puzzled.

'Oh,' he laughs. 'You wonder why they are all women?'

That wasn't actually what I was thinking at all. There is a lot of weirdness about the whole group, and being women isn't really the most weird. I can't quite get why someone from Africa wanted to come here for a picnic. But it seems best just to nod.

'It's something to do with a problem in their country, women's problem, need women to deal with it,' he says.

That makes perfect sense. Women's problems. Mum has told me about women's problems. 'Periods' she called it and told me about the bleeding and how awful it was. Awfulness depends on what else is happening to you. Menstruation sounds pretty good to me, because it frightens men away, she said. Obviously, menstruation was so horrendous in their country that they need armed soldiers to deal with it. I look at them. I think some of them do speak a little English. One rolled her eyes at the man's words and gave a slight shake of her head. So perhaps they didn't shoot girls in their country when they have their periods. My mind is whirring seriously. It's only the cheese sandwich keeping me from running, that and the KitKat.

The man explains a bit more. They had been training to sneak up on the bridge without being detected. That's why they had been wearing the camouflage to make them look like bushes. The man had spotted them, so they'd failed. It meant they needed to try it again somewhere else.

I show him my map, and he explains a lot more. Explanations mean more questions from him. I'm not doing well under interrogation. But suddenly he checks his watch and there isn't any more time for talk.

'Have to be off, get this lot back to camp.' He jumps up and shouts, 'Bye,' as he leads them off. 'Come on you lot. Tomorrow see if you soldiers can sneak up on me down at Cranmere.'

I watch them march away. They've taken off the bushes and stuffed the camouflage outfits into their packs. Soon they start singing as they march away. A beautiful sound, although I can't understand a word. I turn to set off back.

I have a sudden thought, unusual for me. Taking out the map I search for this place "Cranmere". I search everywhere. Cranmere? I can't find it and the rain starts. I go back to the house; it's quite a long way.

Tonight is a Lester day. Lester night. Lester pain.

But this time I have Dartmoor with me. This time I have an army of women soldiers marching over the boggy ground, singing. Wind and their song fill my mind while the fixed good girl smile gets me fewer bruises. I don't think Lester sees the moor. I don't see Lester. I see something wonderful out there, outside this room, this place. And when I do look at him, I think I see a little change. I hope I see a little change. I murmur the words he's told me to say. But at the end I whisper, 'Dartmoor.'

He throws me across the room.

'What did you say?' he screams, loud enough to bring Mum down from heroin heaven.

'Nothing,' I say with a down-turned head and definitely no smirk.

'You did,' he shouts as Mum comes into the room.

'What did she say?' Mum asks him.

Lester is unsure. Lester mumbles. The face of my torturer slips. He is pathetic. Mum sees it. She waves me away and goes to him. 'I'm sure it was nothing.' Her voice is almost soothing. 'Make you a cup of tea,' she adds and takes money out of his wallet while Lester recovers.

Because Lester can't bear to hear me saying the word I said. Lester can't take Dartmoor.

nine

I have taken one of the few light bulbs. I smuggled it away from another room. The broken glass in the lamp in my room was the result of my throwing things around times. Lucky the lamp still works with a new bulb. In the light I search the map.

There it is. Cranmere Pool. Underneath it says, "Letterbox". I have no idea what that means. It's miles out on the moor. Couldn't send a postman out there, could they? Maybe they do. I tell Mouse about the postman striding across black peat and bog, slipping over into Cranmere Pool, getting all the letters soggy, scrabbling around to get them back into the postbag. Mouse and I giggle, sort of snigger, almost laugh.

I slap my hand over my mouth. I made a sound. Did Lester hear it? Turn out the light. Mouse goes under the pillow; it's not a good hiding place. Is he coming down the hallway to my room? I screw my eyes up tight. Then I remember that's no protection. Protection isn't there. Don't protect yourself. He likes resistance, he can hurt me more. Best to let it happen. Think of the moor. He doesn't arrive but the bed is wet again. I move to a drier patch. Can't sleep. Light on again and back to the map.

Early morning comes. I have slept. Lester's car leaving has woken me. I make for the kitchen. I am hungry, Dartmoor has made me hungry again. I eat a tin of potatoes from the cupboard. It has a picture of an old tractor on it. It was probably a modern tractor when the tin was made. But it's not too bad. I need my strength for today.

I pick out some more of the old lady's clothes. Big grey knickers and more. Anything is better than my good girl uniform. Mum has bought me more of the pink and frilly stuff. Probably smells of pee now, like my room. No windows that open.

In the kitchen I find a plastic bottle for water, a coke bottle which came with a pizza, and another tin of whatever. I stuff them into an ancient green shoulder bag. There are sugar lumps in the bottom of it, mostly crusty and broken. I still might eat them.

Mum comes in. She's got that red-eyed pre-injection fury. 'What are you doing? What are you wearing? Where are you going?' She machine-guns her words at me.

I pick up one of Lester's empties. One of a pile mixed with pizza boxes and other rubbish.

'And you can help me clean this up,' Mum shouts.

I throw the bottle at the wall: 'Clean it yourself,' says the brave bad girl and I run. I slow to unlock the door. Mum doesn't come after me, there's something more important to her than a fight over clearing up things. Something she always needs more badly than anything. Certainly, more badly than me.

I'm out on the moor. Sunshine and blue sky. A day to run and run. A day to make for Cranmere Pool and the Letterbox. A day to creep up on some soldiers. A day for a game. Come on Mouse.

o

It rains. This is not normal rain. In all my long, long, supposed, nine and a bit years I have never met rain like this, or even in the later non-existent years that would make me less of an asset. It is not coming down from the sky. It is coming straight at me blown by a gale. The water slices into the old lady's coat. It's a good coat but nothing can withstand this. It is a nasty Lester type of rain. I'm out on the moor and wet and miserable and that's why I think of him again. So I run. My map tells me to make for a farm. I've seen it before down in a valley. A patch of green in the grey of the moor. Another isolated house. I don't want to go too near. I don't think Lester is alone in this world. There are others like him and maybe one of them lives in this farm. Mouse is hiding in a plastic bag I found, deep in the bag on my shoulder.

But I can't see where I'm going, so I have to stick to the path. I'm trying to run, which is difficult, but then I'm going downhill and the rain's behind me. Easier and not so wet. I stumble run on. There's a stream ahead. More like a river today. How can I get across? I have to look at my map. Weirdly I have not noticed that the rain has been turned off. Just stopped. Like a tap. No rain. No wind. I pull out my map. I don't need to cross the river. I go around the side. There's a sort of path again. Now I can see that the farm is the other side of the water, away from me. I'm happier.

The rain comes back. Not so hard this time but just as miserable. I've noticed it comes with the clouds. One moment you're standing in clear air then this huge black monster looms over you and drops a ton of water before going on its way to find someone else to soak. I never knew clouds were so nasty.

Did I say that out loud, because the winds changed, and the last cloud is coming back to get me. I really do run, waste of time, I can't get any wetter.

Stupidly I'm starting to enjoy this. If I had a home, I would have given up this trip and headed for a nice warm bath, crumpets and a fire (even though summer must be here). But I don't. Never had a home like that. I could run back to be beaten senseless and then having to... no, I will never let that into my head while I'm on the moor. I will never go back over the things he makes me do. If I do, it's like it happens over again. Molly, do not think about him. Think about the African soldiers. My soldiers who I'm going to surprise. On I go.

And on.

And on.

I drink from the bottle and eat some of the tin of what turns out to be tomatoes. Squidgy tomatoes. Hope I do meet the soldiers and they give me something. Daft idea really. Will they be out here in the rain and cold? I've not seen anybody since I left the house. No one else is mad enough to be out here today. I think it's Monday.

I come to some sort of building. It's not a house, it's a box-like thing with grass growing on top. At the front there is a large rusty green metal door. This is a locked-up place of concrete. The wind is stronger, but it does seem to blow the clouds away before they get me. I shelter behind a wall and check the map again. I've no real idea where I am. I need some sort of where are you app for the phone which I don't have because I'm not allowed one. The soldier man did ask me if I had a compass. Not knowing what a compass was and not wanting to be stupid I said, 'Of course.' It seemed that a compass was like the "find you" phone app but without the phone. I need one. On the map there are things called observation posts. Am I at one? A place you could sit in and watch, there isn't anyone in it now, is there? I bang on the metal door, no reply.

How many of these have I passed already? I just go on when the rain turns to drizzle. The map says there should be another observation post just before I need to turn off this path. I don't find it. Now I'm going uphill. The ground changes to black bog. Sludge, sludge. I fall over. I'm covered in black mud. I'm running out of energy. I sit on a stone just off the path. I may just have to lie down and give up.

But I don't want to die when I'm out here. This is my own playground. I hear a noise. There are people coming. It's not my soldiers. There are four of them walking towards me. They're laughing, walking quickly, they've all got on the real gear for this weather. They walk straight past me, no stopping, no hellos or questions. Nothing. Then I realise I'm better camouflaged than yesterday's soldiers. I may not be carrying a bush on my back but covered in mud I look like the moor. I'm invisible! I've got superpowers. Don't think I'd be invisible in Lester's kitchen. There, I've ruined it again, brought it back into my mind. I turn into the wind, try to let Dartmoor blow the thoughts away and it works. I follow the walkers. They don't look back. I see them pointing. We are near the top of a hill. Could be anywhere. No chance of finding directions out here.

The walkers have stopped. There's something weird. They are standing next to a pile of rocks and one is balanced on another, just about to fall. I watch them try to pull it down. They can't.

'Pull harder,' I hear one shout.

They're laughing again and then they walk on. I have to see

this. I walk over to the rocks. How does this rock stay there? It should fall over, but it doesn't, and I can't move it, even with my superpowers. I sit again, finish the tomatoes and look at the map. Now I can see where I am because there's a place labelled Hangingstone Hill, and this must be the place. Couldn't name these stones anything else. They're hanging. Looking at Mickey, soggy Mickey who is probably only splashproof, tells me I have been walking for nearly four hours. I've no idea what time the soldiers might get to Cranmere Pool. I can see on this map that there was a much easier route to get to where I am, which is not where I'd wanted to be, but this may be brilliant because Hangingstone Hill is not far from this pool and the Letterbox. Just over there.

And now the sun comes out. It's warm and I think I know where to go. Over there. I'm not looking, trip again, bump to the ground and feel Lester's bruises hit the ground. More mud. It may not be far, but the ground seems to have swallowed up all the rain and now is throwing it back up again. Black vomit even if it is sunny. I should go back to the easier route. I don't want to.

In the distance I hear a whistle. I have to believe it is my army. Because in my mind that is what they are. I just need to get them to march up to Lester's house and shoot him. Would that work? If they shot him would I be free? Or would Mum find another one? Blot that out Molly. This is your game. I crouch down and watch. This is definitely my game. I want to get to them before they spot me. I won't have anyone telling me that creeping up on a group of armed soldiers is a bad idea. They were nice to me before. I'd creep up on anyone who was nice to me. It's unusual. Not the creeping because I do a lot of that.

I see them. Moving bushes across the moor. Moving wet bushes, I expect. They're crossing the bog. If the whistle has gone does that mean Ivan, I think that was his name, has spotted them, like he did before? Now I can see there are two groups. One must have been caught because they are standing up and walking together. The others are still crawling across the ground. They are all making towards a point. If I'm right that's Cranmere Pool. I hurry on. I'm small. I don't need to crawl. I'm the colour of mud, I'm part of the moor. You'll never spot me. I watch the second group get caught. I hear Ivan's laugh. They all stop and swing their backpacks to the ground. I hope it's lunchtime and there's something left for me. A picnic in the Dartmoor sun. I think that could be rare. Now I crawl through grassy stuff, don't mind the damp, the pools of black mud. I'm nearly there. They are all sitting in a circle. There's a gas-cooking thing in the middle. I think they must be making tea or something. Do they have tea in Africa? I must ask.

I've crawled right into their circle, along a sort of ditch. No one else is in here because it stinks of rotting something. Might be sheep. There were some sheep. Has one died in this ditch? Yuck. I touch something slimy, jump to my feet with a small scream. It's the end of my game.

Suddenly there are twenty or so guns pointed at me. I stick my hands up. Isn't that what you are meant to do? Then they all laugh.

'Came up on us better than you lot,' Ivan points at the soldiers and smacks me on the shoulder. It's a kindly gesture but I still flinch. A puzzled look comes over his face, but he doesn't ask. Doesn't ask if there's some old injury on my shoulder, doesn't ask how I got it. I wouldn't tell him even if he did. I'm a good girl. But I don't have to be very good now.

'You eat,' says one of the women, passing me a metal tray of food. It's stew and hot. Something magical made it hot, Ivan tells me. Magic army tricks.

I stuff it in my mouth and listen to them talking. Trying out English, a new language for them all. I get braver.

'You know… yesterday,' I start.

'Yes,' Ivan nods. 'Go on.'

'You asked me if I had a compass.' I sniff. 'Well, I don't, and I don't know what one is.'

Ivan has that serious grown-up look on his face. I've asked the wrong thing. I know that I have given myself away.

He starts off, 'How did you get here? Where do you live? Where are your parents? Do they know you are out here?'

I jump up and run, dropping my tin of stew. I make about three steps when strong arms lift me in the air. One of the soldiers has taken me up in her arms. As she lowers me back to the ground, she shakes her head and says, 'Non,' again or something like that. Ivan has his mouth open. I can see he wants to ask the questions again. All the women seem to join in. I don't understand what they are saying but Ivan shrugs his shoulders and doesn't ask more questions.

'You not need to talk,' the lifting soldier says. 'We come from places where you don't talk.'

I think back to what Ivan had told me about the women needing to sort things out in their country. Women's trouble. I could feel that they understood. Looking into her eyes I could see something familiar. Something I'd seen before. Seen before in a mirror. Pain.

I sit back down and rescue my tin of stew from the mud. There are no more questions, just eating, and they do have tea. I want to stay with them. Why hadn't I answered Ivan's questions? I could have told him everything. No one could stop these soldiers. They could rescue me. They could rescue Mum from Lester. They could creep up to our house and smash their way in before Lester could even get to the poker. They were getting better at creeping. I'd heard Ivan say how much better they were today. I don't trust myself to do this, I know it would go wrong.

Instead, I look around. We are in a sort of dip in the moor. Surrounded by tangles of spiky plants with yellow flowers and softer purple stuff. Further away there is a lot of mud. Trampled mud that suggests that other people come here. Why? There's a sort of box thing. Of course, it's the Letterbox, isn't it? I want to ask Ivan about it, but that could start all the questions again, so I keep quiet.

I hear more voices and look round. It's the four walkers I saw before. They wave at us and we all wave back but they keep their distance; maybe the guns put them off although Ivan says they aren't actually loaded, just being carried for exercise. The walkers are making for the box. They stop and bend down, opening it. I don't have to ask; my African women are just as puzzled. Soon we are all crowding around the box. Ivan doesn't know a lot about it so one of the four walkers does the explanation.

'This was the first Letterbox,' she says. 'There are hundreds over the moor. Most are quite hard to find.'

'Is there a postman? Does a postman come here?' Excited words escape from my mouth. I give myself away; I'm a small girl out here alone.

'Not really, but if you leave a letter with a postage stamp the next person to come here should take it and put it in a real post box,' she says. I see there is more she wants to say. 'We saw you over at Hangingstone. You must be careful, there's deep bogs on the moor, someone can easily fall in and drown.'

That's only the start. She has a nosey adult look about her. Before she launches into a full interrogation, the soldiers surround her. Ivan is translating their own rapid-fire questions. One of the walkers speaks a bit of their language so they're well into talking. I escape with nothing about me given away.

The woman goes on, 'Inside.' She bends down and picks something out of the box. 'There's a rubber stamp in every box. You bring your own ink pad.' She pulls out a tin from her pocket. In it is a black pad. She shows us how to use the stamp.

'There, Cranmere Pool.' She holds up a piece of paper with the mark that gives the name of this place. 'All the boxes have different stamps.'

The pages of her notebook are covered in stamps of all sizes. Many are animal heads but there are loads of weird shapes as well.

'We walk over the moor and collect them,' another of the walkers explains, and he's got a book of stamps as well.

We all want a go, finding bits of paper. I've a scrap in the pocket, a bit damp, so the woman tears off a piece of her paper and gives me a fresh stamp. I can see she is about to return to her questions.

Ivan steps in and moves us all off. 'Back to work,' he snaps, in an army sort of voice, but gives me a wink as we move away. The walkers leave on their own route; as they do our soldiers are examining their pieces of paper and seem to find it all quite funny. Ivan says they can't believe that someone doesn't steal the stamps.

When they all stand up, ready to march back to their camp, I'm still staring at my scrap of paper. The moor, this place, the walkers, the soldiers, the Letterboxes – all part of a strange world that I've found. None of these people have hurt me or done… that to me. I suppose this is normal life. I can't see my stamp now. My eyes are watering. I want this to be my forever, even if the rain is starting again to hide my tears.

I will do it tomorrow. I will meet them again and tell them why I hurt all over. Tell them about Lester… about Mum, I suppose. I'll do it. They will save me; I know they will.

'Bet I can sneak up on you again tomorrow,' I said bravely to Ivan.

'Bet you can't,' he smiled back.

'Can.'

'Not unless you follow us to Africa. It's back there for all of us tomorrow. Training finished, real work in the bad lands.'

My moment has gone. The air disappears around me. I have dared to hope when I should not have hoped. They can hurt me. I run. I hear their calls, but they disappear on the wind. I never did find out about the compass. I have no one to send a letter. I run faster.

I stop running when I get back to the track up Oke Tor. Looking back there is nothing to see. A bleary mist has rolled down from the higher tors, smothering the view. Can I catch a bit of the soldiers singing? Maybe they all fell into a bog, drowned like the lady said. I try not to want that because I know that is the real forever creeping up, the forever hating everything.

Ahead I see a shadow coming up the steep side of Oke Tor. Another walker? Another person with questions I really can't answer. Another person to let me down. I run again all the way to Belstone Tor and there I stop for breath. Why am I hurrying? Not to get back to a nice dry home! I know I have been out too long. Too long not to miss trouble. And I don't.

'Where have you been, Mol?' Mum is trying to stand between me and the furious-looking Lester. He pushes her away.

Tonight is the worst night it has ever been. He hurts me all over. He does all the things Nat told me they do in the forever that doesn't have any Letterboxes or walkers. But it doesn't take it all away. With each hurt I think of Dartmoor. As it gets worse, I pull the picture of the rain-soaked moor into my head. Lester sees the blankness in my face.

I know he hates me for being out on the moor. There is something out there that frightens him. I like that, I want to frighten him. But he wants to take that away. He hates my blankness when he wants to see me hurting.

'You little slut,' he shouts. 'I will make you cry.' He takes the cigarette from his mouth and stubs it out on my chest. I start to scream but he grabs my head and clamps his hand over my mouth.

'Cry, you bastard.' He tries to snarl but it sounds like whining.

The pain is going. I have reached the Hangingstones in my head. The balanced rocks are in my mind. I can't cry. Lester throws me to the floor. He looks confused. I hope he's run out of bad things to do.

Then he tells me to remember the whistle. 'I blow it, you run. If you're not here immediately you know what I'll do.' It is his way of breaking me from the moor, controlling everything.

I am rather dazed so I look confused. He picks up the poker. 'Your mum won't walk again.' He's braver now. 'Got that?'

I nod. But it's not enough. I am back to having to call him

Daddy and saying I'll be a good girl. Just to make sure he gives me a playful smack with the poker. Playful for him. I won't be using that leg for a while. He lets me leave for my room.

On the bed I pull out the stamped piece of paper. I see the words of Cranmere Pool and then I cry.

ten

More days, more Lester, no soldiers and no time on the moor. I am near to asking Mum for something to help, some of what she uses to escape.

'Go for it,' Nat used to say. 'Why fight it? It'll get you one day.'

Was Nat on drugs? I think I'd seen her smoke some weed, but not inject. Had her life started to take her to the forever that my mum lived? I really don't want that to happen. I want Nat to get to be old and brave, tell the tales but don't live the life. It's not what she said would happen, but I want her to be different. She was scary, and I want that to mean braver. Has she got away? Will anyone get away?

Yes.

I will not let the soldiers disappear, at least not in my mind. I wish I hadn't run away. Why had I decided to wait before telling them? In this house I know the answer. I wasn't ever going to tell them. I wasn't going to tell anyone because telling them would bring a whole pile of mess. I haven't even told Mouse, even though she knows. None of what happens here is real to anyone else. Those people out on the moor. They didn't know. If I told them would they put their arms around me, hug me, take me home? Lester has made me dirty. Tell anyone and they'd see the dirt. It would make me the girl it happened to. That would be a new forever and I don't like it.

If this is to stop, then I am the only person who can do it. Is that what I have to do?

Before I take on the world, Mum comes into the room. I'm on the bed. I'm still on the bed because in this house there is no other place for me. Mum walks out of the room. That's not unusual. Mum walks back in and out.

'Stop,' I shout.

She's back in. 'What?'

I sit up. 'Nothing,' then, 'tell me.'

'He's late,' she says and sits down, near but not too near. I guess that's because she knows what I am about to say. Doesn't stop me.

'Brilliant, later the better.'

I can see that neither of those wonderful bits of non-Lester are good for Mum. She does more of the in-room out-room restless march before there's a shout at the front door. No need to knock. Mum shivers, she knows the voice, and tells me to stay still and 'shut it'. No one good ever comes to our door. I listen. Murmured voices and one is very deep, a sound that echoes. It makes me shiver too, and I haven't even seen him.

Back in, Mum says, 'Got to go, back soon.'

And I don't shut it, which doesn't matter because Mum and Mister with the murmured voice have gone as well. I feel that some of this is good because it may mean something has happened to Lester. Something like, squashed by a huge digger, eaten by a snake, chopped to pieces by a mad butcher, poisoned by a murdering drug dealer, but not dead of old age. I just didn't guess that he'd been put in jail.

I don't get all the story in one go. Mum lets pieces out between eye-rolling episodes of near overdose.

'We'll be fine.' She grins in a sort of way that isn't a grin but something that I think zombies do. 'Fine.' It's Mum's victory grin which lets me know it is the opposite of fine. Her victories never last.

What she means is that Lester has been caught doing whatever he does with the garage man, who doesn't get caught and turns out to be the one who was murmuring at the door. When Mum tells me about him she shivers again. I think Mum may have met him on one of her working nights. He came up to tell her the news. Gave her Lester's car along with his instruction to 'shut it or else'. And I just know he will be another poker-wielding man.

Mum believes that's fine. Lester's in jail. 'Don't have to be a good girl,' she says as though that's another of her victories. A victory she wants to claim. Along with having the car and the real victory is she knows where Lester keeps his cash.

I am young and stupid, but I know about people being put in jail. I've met people who have been put in jail. Those people have been frequent visitors to the places we've lived in for short times. And why have they been visitors? It's because after being put in jail they let them out. And I just know how happy Mr Lester will be to find Mum has spent all his hard-stolen money and she lies waiting for him on the floor in a near-permanently chemical-induced non-human state.

'We've got to get out.' I shake her.

'Fine.' She's giggling.

'Out, get up, get out.' I'm frantic.

'Fine.'

I get nowhere. Later her phone goes. Picking up the last bits of signal. It's a text and Mum dances as she reads it but doesn't speak. I read it later.

Mum does more crazy giggles. 'He's been done for the last job, found guilty, he'll get months.'

Mum makes out how happy she is and how wonderful it will be. 'Just us together.'

I tell her. It's no good. No togetherness and no chance of ever being happy.

We do get time. Mum buys some food. A routine develops. Sometimes Mum takes drugs, at other times Mum takes drugs. I am nowhere and it is only me that knows that this is just waiting. It is only me that knows how bad it will be when Lester gets back. Telling Mum we need to get out of here quickly is useless.

'Go back to the garage and ask that man when Lester is going to get out.' I know I am whining.

'He's gone,' Mum says, and she is on some smooth carpet ride across the sky – or that's what she seems to be telling me.

'Ask someone else?' There are no magic carpets here.

'Later,' she smiles.

It takes a few days before I go out again with Lester in jail. Partly because of the huge bruised lump on my leg which hurts just to stand. But I'm slow to go out again because I can't take the same happening, meeting the normal world and then having it taken away. But I have to go. The moor pulls me too hard. I only have to take a few steps before I feel like someone else. That's my drug.

Today I have studied the map and want to race up Cosdon Beacon and find something the map calls a stone circle. I set off. There are more people about, and children. I think it must be school holidays, they look happy. I would keep away, but the map says I should go through the village and I sort of want to. The day is clear but there's nearly always dampness in the air, so I get away with having my green hood up and could still pass for an old walking person. But I get hellos from people I pass, weird, wouldn't happen in London, easier to hide away there. I just know if I stop the questions will start. I hurry on past a pub. There are no shops here and I'm soon onto grass and heading away downhill from the village.

Below me I can hear the stream. It's a blue line on the map. I love that. It's like I have discovered it for the first time, my stream, my adventure. I can hear more noise, more children. I get to the stream and see them playing, jumping running shouting laughing shrieking. I stand and watch with a smile starting, one small girl slips and falls, she cries. I start forward but stop as an adult appears and lifts her away. It is a tender moment; she gets a hug. I hate her. Then I try not to hate her. I walk on up the hill on the other side, telling myself all sorts of things that make no real sense.

I walk to a tune. Some nursery rhyme that loses any meaning as I scramble the words. I am trying to blot out that feeling of hate. I want to be picked up from danger. The little girl in the stream wasn't in danger, didn't need to be rescued. I do. It is so hard to shake off that hate, Nat's hate, the forever hate. 'Humpy dumpy sat on a nail, Humpy dumpy started to wail.' Walk on, push on, up the hill, push Molly push. I pant. There are fewer people now but more curious.

'Out here alone?' a man calls as he crosses the path in front of me.

'No,' I mutter.

He's sort of standing in my way. It's not a Lester sort of look that he has on his face, but an interfering look.

'Not safe out here on your own.' He speaks firmly, as though he's guessed my good girl age.

I hang my head. What does he know about safe places? I think about running but I know he'll grab me. He's that sort of person, probably a teacher or something. I know what he will say next.

'Where are your parents?' And he does.

Where should I start? I live with a… my mum's a… dad? I never knew him… now piss off and let me walk. Those are the words I'd like to say but I won't, I'm not saying anything. I start to feel my body shiver; it's not cold but I don't know what to do. My eyes are starting to sting. I will fall down. I must leave. I run. One step before he grabs my arm. Another man appears, two women, we've a crowd now. I struggle.

'There you are,' cries out a voice.

I twist in the arm-hold and turn to the sound. Map Woman. Where did she come from?

'She being a nuisance?' The woman steps up. I am released.

'No,' the man laughs. 'Thought she was lost.'

'Went ahead too fast for me.' Map Woman laughs as well.

They are all having a little laugh. I walk off, hoping to be forgotten.

'Hang on, not so fast.' Map Woman comes after me, calling thanks to the other walkers who march off.

I speed up.

'Wait.'

I don't like this. She has to have been following me, where from? Does she know where I live? Does she know how I live? There is something wrong about her, something that isn't quite

Lester but not far away. Has he sent her to watch me? I could outrun her. She is not quick, but she still comes after me. I could run. I wait.

'Much easier if you walk with me,' she speaks and carries on walking up the hill, slow but the look on her face tells me she will walk this hill and more.

I follow. We make ridge after ridge, the path seems to disappear and reappear; the moor is still damp and I tread in wet holes but we keep on and there is no more talking, yet. We reach the top where stones have been built up into a large pile.

'That's the beacon.' She points and explains.

I love the moor and I listen to her while she describes how fires were lit across the country in olden times to warn of war and stuff. Then I drift off, there can be too much – who is this woman? I don't ask. Something about her makes me not want to know. I'm expecting her to tell me everything, and I don't think it is going to be good. I thought she'd tell me after the beacon stuff, as though she had been warming up to it.

But she doesn't. She brings out some sandwiches and we eat them. Why this woman should share her lunch with me I have no idea. Then when I think she is about to start her story, she jumps up.

'Better get down.' She points back to the village and we are off again.

I don't say anything about the stone circle, it's in the opposite direction. I think I may get another lecture and I want it to be my stone circle if I ever find it. By now I sort of want her to go, she is sticky, stands too close, walks too close, keeps looking as though she has something to say and isn't sure whether to tell me. Like a shadow. It makes me feel uncomfortable.

Eventually we wander down the same path we had come up, just as boggy. The sun disappears and there are no children playing in the stream when we cross the bridge to go back up the hill to the village.

'Bye, then,' she says as we reach the road, and with a wave she is off.

Perhaps I should run after her and shout questions, pour out my story, ask for help. It feels like she may know it all already. I trudge back to the house, the one that might be Lester's house or his aunt's. No one had missed me. I was hungry.

Chicken nuggets.

eleven

I suppose even chicken nuggets are food. I eat and think. I think about the questions I didn't ask the Map Woman. These questions still rumble in my mind. Who, why, what and so on. Why I didn't ask them should be important; somehow it isn't. It can't be coincidence that she pops up behind me on the moor. I don't think even the first time I met her or when she gave me the map were chance meetings. That means she's been watching, watching me. Is she part of Lester's world? She must have something to do with it.

That has to be the reason I didn't ask. I don't want to know that she has something to do with Lester. This is my Dartmoor, mine, and I don't want him to follow me out there or send someone. If she'd told me that Lester had sent her it would ruin everything. I tense, my hands grip the knife, I plunge a fork into the last nugget. At least if I don't know, then I can pretend she doesn't belong in that side of my life. Who am I kidding? I don't have another side to my life. Lester is my life.

I still sort of want to know. Couldn't she be a fairy godmother? No.

I don't see much of Mum that night. So I can't tell her of

the day's sights and smells. Map Woman sort of unmagicked the top of Cosdon Beacon. But the view was still special. I have that in my head, miles and miles of moor. If I had looked the other way it would have felt more normal, houses and roads. But I am a one-way looking girl. I only see the moor and it takes everything else away, at least for a while, or a moment, or a second. I want to tell Mum. If she sees the things I've seen, then it would make her change, she wouldn't be able to avoid it.

'Mum,' I call, making for the stairs with a definite purpose, a plan to tell her about the world outside, perhaps take her with me.

She's in the toilet throwing up. Maybe it was the nuggets. She does throw up quite a lot. I guess it's the drugs. Don't suppose she'd be interested in what I saw. My purpose and my plan drift away.

I go to bed, aching from the walk, but it's a good ache not a Lester ache. And I sleep after a little chat to Mouse. She understands why the moor is so important.

Mum wakes early. I hear her. Should I try to talk again? Mum leaves in the car. No message.

I have to do something. I decide to hide anything interesting to eat in case I, or even we, need it. That means tins of beans, tomatoes or stew. Then I do a bit more searching around the house. It isn't easy. The house has the creaks and groans of a person and every one of them makes me think he's back. I want to hide. DON'T hide Molly, it is so much worse when he finds you, he doesn't want to think you are a person who decides things. You are an object. Don't hide but look around.

I find that if I stand on a chair, I can see the moor out of an upstairs window. There isn't much to see because the trees have grown up almost to cover everything, but I can see a little way. And what do I see? It's Map Woman. She's looking up at the house, from out towards the flagpole. I almost fall off the chair, did she see me? Why is she there? I can only guess she's waiting for me, spying on me.

I move away. There are so few things in this house. There must have been four bedrooms, five if you count the boxish room at the top of the stairs. But only Mum's room has a bed. The rest are empty, dusty and empty. There are marks in the dust so some bits of furniture must have been there once. No curtains at the windows. The shutters are outside and some of them are closed but they still let in shafts of light through cracks in the wood. All of this makes me scared. I go back downstairs, stopping again as a gust of wind hits the windows and it sounds like someone coming in.

I keep away from Lester's corner of the kitchen. I see that space too often and I'm going to walk on back to the room I've been given. I stop. There is a small door in the wall above his bed. Like another cupboard. It's in the radioactive place – Lester's mattress in the corner. I turn and take a step towards it. I stop. I turn again and take a step away. I have not taken a breath, makes me dizzy. It's dangerous. I listen for anything but hear only the wind and rain which has started again. I am going to do this.

I step over Lester's mattress. I almost don't make it with my legs going to jelly. I can feel him, this brings back things in my head, a flashback that jumps to his commands: do this; do that. I grab for the cupboard door, pull it open. Papers fall out. The cupboard is full of them. Was full of them until I opened the door. Now a pile of them have scattered. I hear the car.

My jumping flashbacks are taken over by panic as the

papers flutter. The car door shuts. Do I hear voices? Has Mum brought Lester back from prison? I can't get the stuff back in the cupboard. Everything I push onto a shelf falls back out. I can hear footsteps. I run to my room.

It's only Mum. I hear her stop in the kitchen. So quiet.

'Molly,' she calls.

I walk back out. If it's only Mum I don't care.

'What's this?' she points and speaks like real mums do.

'No idea,' I say, because I haven't.

'You'd better tidy it up.' The "in case Lester comes back and sees it" is felt but not said.

'Tidy it yourself,' I say with arms crossed. I am not going to win this, but a shouted fight would be good, just to find out that Mum is still not a dead person on the move.

Mum has been staring at the papers, reading and not dead at all. This cupboard is not where Lester stores his cash. He keeps that in the toilet cistern – Mum says he learnt that from a film – and when I looked last time a lot of it had gone. I guess that's why Mum hadn't bothered to search this cupboard before. She only needs cash, not paperwork. But something has caught her eye; she's reading. For this to hold her attention it must mean she sees something to help her habit. This is going to be great for Lester. Mum's taken all your drugs, pinched your cash and is now planning something catastrophic. I like the word but not the idea – catastrophe and Mum fit so well together.

I move closer to get a better look. There are some old certificates or something. I see Lester's name on one of the old ones. It says it's a certificate of something. There's another official-looking document. Mum starts to stare into the distance, almost as though she's found something new – like thinking. It's a bad idea. When she thinks she always comes up with things that don't work. Like coming here. Mum thinking and the missing money are both bad. We should get out now, in the car or anything, but Mum has other plans. You can almost hear her mind clicking away.

'We'll be all right,' she says. Her words could be for me, but I think it's just her that expects to be all right.

She stuffs the papers back into the cupboard.

'Don't tell anyone.' And those words are for me.

Who would I tell? When she says that I realise she knows Lester will be coming back. Worse. I think she believes she has found something that will change everything when he returns. I think Lester will pick up the poker when he finds the money has gone. I do not believe Mum has found anything that will stop him breaking her legs. But I know that she has made up her mind and thinks she can work this out, make it right for her.

'Make it right for you,' she says with blurred confused happiness.

I have heard her say that it will be all right so many times before. It never is all right.

At least she's brought back pie and chips.

We eat.

Mum has a "lie down". I look at my map and think about the woman. I wonder if she is still outside, staring up at the house. Planning whatever it is she is going to do.

o

I wake early. I hear the sound of birds. I can imagine them outside. I want to be outside. I will go. I stuff a couple of tins into my bag, or at least my borrowed-from-the-old-lady bag. I imagine her giving me instructions.

'Don't forget to take some water, Molly,' she says as I fill the old plastic coke bottle.

'Make sure you go to the loo,' she instructs, because there aren't many places out there to hide and crouch. I don't flush in case it wakes Mum. I am on a secret mission to the stone circle.

I leave and it's only just light. I check in case Map Woman is about, but there's no one, only sheep. I can just see where I need to go. There is a path down to the stream in the valley. I hurry off. I am not walking to my nursery rhyme. I only need that when I go uphill. Soon I am down onto the flat ground, hills on both sides. Daylight is stronger now and it is hard to take my eyes off the sparkling water. It just bounces along over the rocks. I find a piece of stick and throw it in, watching it dash away and I run back after it.

'Wait for me, stick,' I say so seriously, but stick doesn't wait and disappears.

I cross over the water. It's some sort of crossing place and it looks as though someone drives across here, there are tyre marks in the mud. Maybe they look after the sheep. Do sheep need looking after? These ones seem to just stay out here and eat grass. But probably everything needs some looking after.

I have seen someone on what looks like a quad bike, racing across the moor, stopping from time to time. But I don't know what he's doing. I have made up lives for the people who live in the village. Sheep man – he's a big hairy man who rides the bike thing. I imagine he'll get fat with all the racing about and not walking. Perhaps he'll get so fat he can't look after the sheep. He'll have a wife, of course, and she'll have to do the sheep work. Bet he won't let her have his quad bike. But that's good because she won't get fat and Mr Sheep man will die and she will be in charge. A lot of the men die in my imagination.

Now I am going uphill. There isn't a track and I have to pick my way carefully to avoid the boggy bits. I remember the warning the Letterbox walker gave me about falling down a hole. I look out for holes but only find squidgy bits. It's not as muddy as Hangingstone Hill. There are more plants here and one or two stumpy trees. I sit under one of them and open a tin. It's not the sort of beans I had expected. These are red and don't taste so good. I think they need cooking.

Could I light a fire and cook them? I've seen some matches in the cupboard. Next time I'll bring some. Or is that a bad idea? Maybe the fire will get out of control and burn across the moor. It might burn the house down. Setting fire to the house may have to be done anyway. I imagine all Lester's papers burning. I imagine Lester burning. Sitting under this tree and looking over this huge place I can almost think about Lester without that sick feeling. The moor is almost big enough to swallow my thoughts. And I have it all to myself, don't I? I feel a prickly feeling on my neck; I look around quickly. There's nothing.

I get up and walk on. I may not have a compass thing, but I have stared at this map over and over. I work out what the brown lines mean, they get close together when it's steep. I think I just have to make for the ridge up ahead. When I reach it there's a broad path. I can see it runs up to the top of Cosdon Beacon. That was the route I was going to take until Map Woman took over. I'm not sure which way to go because I don't know exactly where I am. The map says I need to go towards something called Hound Tor, and I think that must be off to the right. The map says it's a tor which I know now means hill but it's not much of a hill. The path is easier than struggling over bog. It is later in the day and there are a few other walkers about in the distance. No one I recognise.

It's there.

That is so weird. Just ahead of me is the stone circle. It couldn't be anything else. Stones seem to have been planted in the moor. They aren't regular ones. It's not a building. Just rocks stuck in the ground – in a circle. Bit like broken teeth. I run into the middle. This is spooky. What is it for? It has to have been made a long time ago. I wish I knew more. Was it made by cavemen? I sit down on the dampish grass and think about cavemen. They'd tramp over the moor carrying huge clubs and chase dinosaurs or some animal to eat. I'd like to think it was a cavewoman who built this circle. Bet she found something better to eat than dinosaur – or chicken nuggets. Must have taken ages to drag these stones here because there aren't any big rocks anywhere near. I lie back and watch the clouds blowing across the sky; they aren't big wet ones. It might even not rain at all today. I wish I hadn't eaten those beans.

'Hello again.'

I have almost jumped into the sky. It's her again. Map woman. How…?

'They used to bury people here, probably killed them here as well.' She launches into another load of information without bothering to give me an explanation of her arrival.

I'm still on the ground wondering whether to leg it. While I'm wondering about that I look her over. She's not scary like Lester although I know there must be some connection. She's pretty much kitted out like the other walkers on the moor. Long green hooded coat over waxy looking trousers – a waterproof outfit. The hood is off, and I'm fixed on her face which is damaged on one side, not that badly but she does keep putting her hand up to cover it when she catches me looking. She is a bit lined and wrinkled, like she's old, but that doesn't fit with her voice which sounds younger. Mousey sort of hair blown wavy in the wind, not the colour of my Mouse. But you can't look away from her eyes, the suspicion and something worse they carry. That's when I remember – I left my Mouse under the pillow.

I jump up. I should get back, move Mouse to a drawer. She's going to be cross with me. I shouldn't have left her on her own. But there are things I want to know.

Map Woman is still going on about the moor and these stones. I get the feeling she's making it up, filling in, stopping my questions.

'Who are you?' I blurt out, thinking she's never going to stop.

Stop she does. Halts right in mid-sentence and turns her head away from me. We're out in this wild bit of the moor, where she says people get killed and buried. The moor has filled my head with new ideas, and I don't want to die when I am out here. I run a few steps, to give me space in case she whips out a knife or something.

'Wait,' she cries, and it's a blubbery sort of call because she's crying now.

I wait. I stand waiting but if you said boo loudly I'd be the other side of the moor before you'd catch me. It's a tense sort of wait, shifting from one foot to another.

'Walk with me?' she asks and somehow we set off, back to the wide path. We're heading away from anywhere. I can see the pointy hill with the box on top of it – Steeperton. It's not such a pointy hill from this side. I'm not sure I want to walk with her to this hill. I wanted this to be just for me one day. I've been thinking about this hill from almost the first time I came on the moor. It's the hill that fixes in my mind when I need to lose what happens with Lester. That man. There has to be some connection with her.

We walk a bit. She's not a quick walker, one leg seems to drag behind. After a bit she sets down on a large stone and points to another close by. I am meant to sit. Is she going to explain or is something much worse going to happen?

'Have you seen any papers?'

I nod because I have, not because I want to tell her; it's automatic. Why am I answering her questions?

'Who are you?' I bleat again. I can't sound stronger. It's the sort of bleat that she can ignore. I am used to having my questions ignored.

'What sort of papers did you see?'

A ray of sunlight escapes the clouds above Cosdon, shining down, highlighting colours of green and purple. It's like a searchlight moving down towards the stream. The moor, my moor, the place that changes me.

I stand. I am brave Molly who has escaped. 'How do you know about the papers, why are you following me, who are you and what do you want?' I say loudly and with a face I think matches my bravery.

She laughs. I want to stamp my feet. I am just as helpless as I have ever been.

'Want a sandwich?' She dives into her backpack and pulls out a neatly wrapped pile of crusty bread with something like ham poking out. Real food. We eat.

'It's my house,' she says to the wind over my shoulder.

And I get an explanation. I am an experienced girl. I know

when someone lies. Or when they tell you less than everything. Which for me is always. She says her name is... Irene. She says it with the sort of pause that makes me think she's just picked that name from the clouds.

'He stole it.' She's talking about the house and she brushes off most of the questions I try to ask. Just ignores them. She's only going to give the story that she wants me to hear.

'It was my mother's.' The house I suppose she means.

'The old lady?' I ask.

'Mum died.' I suppose her not answering may mean the same as agreeing.

'He didn't kill her?'

'And he just started selling off all the furniture and anything else he could get money for.'

I might as well just listen. It is a story. I will have to think about it later. Go over her words and see which ones I think are true. She tells me she was married to Lester. She goes off track when she says that and starts shouting. That's the only bit I'm certain is true. Lester makes you want to lose it. There's a lot more about her mum, how she loved the moor, loved walking everywhere. Loved the ponies.

'Ponies?'

That's an easier question for her. She explains about the woolly animals I keep seeing.

'Dartmoor ponies, they let them wander out here to feed themselves, belong to the horse traders, not always well looked after. Mum used to feed them when the weather turned to cold.'

Oh, so running after things that don't get well looked after and feeding them runs in her family. I think that, while she goes on about other animals on the moor. It's hard to keep interested but I want to find out more from her. I don't know why I should. Most things I find out don't end up being good.

Was she really married to Lester? Did she know what he did to girls like me? Was I going to ask her that? Again – NO. If I ask it means I'm telling her what happens to me. She'll look at me with different eyes. I will disgust her. I'm disgusting to have let that happen. Her eyes will wander over me, imagining what he does, even without the details she will make up the worst in her mind, won't she? That's what I'd do. For her, I would become just as disgusting as Lester is. I think she knows.

'One of the papers should be Mum's will.' Her voice breaks into my thoughts; have I missed much? She goes on, 'She would have left everything to me. Lester says it belongs to him as my husband. That's not what Mum wanted. She hated him.'

So-called Irene drifts off. She's staring out at the hills. There are more walkers below us. One group pass us by with cheery hellos. I don't get interrogated while I am with Irene. So that's one quite good thing. Also, I am liking her mum even more now I know she hated Lester. But I am bored with all the stuff Irene is going on about. I am not out here for lectures.

'Can we go?' I stand up and I'm going to go whatever she does. She looks surprised.

'Can you look for it?' She joins me on the path.

'Eh?' I have lost the thread of this.

'The will?' she pleads. 'It'll say it's a will and have Mum's name on it – Doris Penworthy. You'll look for it? Please?'

What I should have said was, 'Yes I'll look for it providing you save my life from that man.' But I don't because sitting down has made me cold and I'm shivering. It may be summer, but the wind is cold. Takes away any sensible thoughts, so

I just mumble, 'Suppose.' And we head off, not aiming for Steeperton but back down into the valley.

This route is much wetter. We hop from one damp grassy lump to another. First it drizzles. The air changes to fog. It comes up so quickly. I knew which way we needed to go to reach the stream. But with trying to keep out of the wettest places I don't know which way we should be going anymore. Somehow, we've come back uphill. You can only see a few feet in front of you. I have been keeping close to Irene.

'Haven't you got a compass?' she asks.

No, I haven't got a compass. I don't say, 'What is a compass?' She pulls one out of her pocket, at least that's what the round disk with a load of numbers and letters on it must be. She shows it to me and it's obvious I haven't a clue. So I get more shivery explanations as we stand and drip because drizzle has turned to rain.

'We want to head north-west,' she says, and shows me how to use the compass. 'That's the way back down to the stream.'

Then she does what I am expecting.

'You will look for it, won't you?'

I stare at her.

'Won't you?'

The   or-else-I-am-going-to-leave-you-out-here-in-the-fog hangs on her words. She's using me. She is a different type of Lester. I know the sort. You just agree with them, so I do. She says, 'Good.' I might have said why don't you do it, why don't you go into your house, your mother's house, and find this will and then throw Lester out? I don't say any of that because I know the answer and I don't want to hear it from her – supposing she told the truth. It's like if you don't say it then you can pretend it doesn't happen, or in her case didn't happen. Because the reason could be all tied up with things about Irene, why her face is damaged and why she walks with a limp. I don't want to test out how that happened in case Lester was the cause. If he can do that to Irene, his wife, then surely, he can do it to Mum. It's not a made-up threat, it's something he's done before. He's had practice.

We walk on.

And she holds the compass out in front of her as we walk. Now we are a bit more in a hurry and just bash through the weather.

There's no more talking. We make the stream. Cross. Up the hill and stop at a gate only a few steps away from Lester's house. Or is it Irene's house?

'Bring it out here, won't you?' She stops, and I know there will be more because she will produce the magic lever to make me want to do it. The reason that she thinks will make me do what she wants. I guess she knows I am not the sort of girl who would do anything without a reason – like a real Nat type of girl.

First, she gives me the compass.

'If you bring the papers to me, then I can get you out of this mess. The thing with Lester. We can get rid of him.' She's not going to say in words what he does, we have to imagine it, too terrible to say and far worse to imagine.

I'm meant to nod and be grateful. What I should be asking is why do I have to search through that dangerous man's private papers before you are going to do the fairy godmother bit and save my life? I don't believe it's going to happen. I nod and look grateful. I will put this with all the other plans that are not going to work. Or telling her that I won't do it because there is always something near a threat coming my way.

twelve

I hear the screams.

Lester is back.

I stop, strength draining from me. I should stay out, run. But I can't. I go on because I hope it will stop when Lester sees I haven't run away, that he will stop when he sees the good girl is back. But this is not about me. There is nothing I can say or do that will change anything. My head is swimming. I knew this would happen.

I have arrived in time to see the garage man just leaving as I come into the kitchen. He is the most enormous man I have ever seen.

'You owe me,' Garage Man shouts, slamming the door, which makes the whole house shake.

o

Mum is on the floor, sobbing and choking to get out words, about getting the money back. Lester is still holding the poker.

'I told you what would happen,' he says, looking at me and raising his arm.

'I haven't done anything,' I yell.

'She has,' Lester sneers.

'NO,' Mum pleads, holding her hand up, hoping to stop him.

'Yes,' Lester gives a sick laugh, before smashing the poker down on her leg, once, twice. I run at him, he hurls me away to the ground and hits her again.

I hear the snap of bone; blood is pouring from the wound. Mum slumps to the floor and doesn't move. Has he killed her? I hear a moan.

Lester turns on me. I wait for the blow. It doesn't come. He grabs me from the floor, shakes me. I try to reach out for Mum.

'Let me go,' I beg, but it is useless.

'Forget about her,' Lester pulls me back. 'She's trash.' He jabs her but she doesn't move. 'And she's stolen my fucking money.'

Lester is holding me tight, and I am numb all over. Is this the end? Are we both going to die?

'Got to get the money back.' Lester drops the poker, lets me go and turns away. 'What… how.' He is talking to himself and falls back into his chair with his head in his hands. 'Must get it back,' he says again and seems to have forgotten me.

I drop down to Mum. Hold on to her. Her body is limp and doesn't move. At least I can see her breathing.

Lester sounds frightened, why? Slowly, I work it out. Lester is out of jail and I guess that means he's done enough time in prison. The garage man must have brought him home and Mum said Lester was scared of the garage man. Now I understand. Lester must have been looking after all the money from their last job. Mum has spent it, spent Garage's money. 'You owe me,' Garage had shouted.

Lester is still muttering 'how' over and over. It seems to go on forever. I don't move from Mum, holding her. I must protect her. I don't know how to do it.

'Got it,' Lester shouts and smacks his thigh. 'Got it,' he says again, and I look up at him, hoping this will mean he isn't going to kill us – yet. He is giving me the sort of look that tells me that nothing is over. It seems that something has switched on in his head. He looks up at me with almost a smile and nods, 'Yes, that's it.'

He gets up and pulls me away from Mum. I struggle but he has his hands at my throat.

'You're not going out there again.' He shakes me, pulls me right up to his face. 'You give me that key.' He rips at my clothes. I still have on the old lady's coat. He finds the key to the moor side door. I watch as he laughs at me. 'Didn't think I knew about that, did you?'

I gaze at him, something makes me think he must be daft, how would I have got out without the key? Gazing isn't enough. He smacks me around the head.

'Did you?'

What am I to say? Think quickly, Molly, before he hits you again.

'No,' I say and it's more a snivel.

It's still not enough. I have to go through the whole daddy routine. It seems to calm him down, but it takes time. Mum starts to moan again. I see Lester look back at the poker.

'No… don't… please don't.' I raise more than a snivel this time. 'We have to get her to hospital,' I say, over and over again, and it makes no difference.

'She's not going anywhere. And neither are you. Not until I get my money back.' Lester picks up Mum's phone. 'Not phoning anyone.' He gives it the poker treatment; the phone disintegrates on the floor.

'I'll be back.' He seems ready to leave, anxious to get on with whatever he has imagined will get the money back.

If he will just go, then I will get help. He sees that in my face.

'Thinking of running off?' Lester snarls. 'Don't. If you try, I'll really smash her up when I come back.'

I'm blank. There must be something I can do when he's gone.

'In fact, I think I'll break her other leg, just to make sure.' He raises the poker again. I'm screaming, 'NO,' and he's laughing and telling me to make sure I don't try anything. I have to promise. I don't do it to his satisfaction.

'Got to keep you pretty,' he says, almost as though he is concerned about me. 'Doesn't mean I have to be nice.' His arm moves back, I see his fist. He hits me in the stomach. I cannot breathe. I am on the floor.

'You'll get it back for me, got to keep you pretty but you'll pay for this.' I get a kick as he leaves.

I gasp. Small sucking noises are all I manage after Lester's blows. I choke on each one. I need more air. Mum is on the floor. I can see where the poker has hit her. I can see the broken bone sticking through the blood. Mum has come round. She is weeping and through the tears she tries to talk.

'I'll make it up, get it all back, just a few days.' Her words make no sense.

Lester returns. I will not get away.

'You couldn't make anything!' Lester stands over Mum, he shouts, he kicks Mum's leg, she howls while Lester shouts, 'You ugly old slag, you never got much before, won't get anything now.'

I try to tell him to stop, but small rasping noises are as loud as I can do. It's enough to make him turn at me. 'Told you I'd make her crawl. Stupid, stupid slag.' He stops to kick her again. 'Stole my fucking money.'

Mum doesn't speak after the next kick, she doesn't move. I try to get to her. It's me that's crawling now. Lester drags me back, throws me across the room. 'Keep away from her. She's filth.'

Lester is about to leave again, he turns, turns back.

'Almost forgot. Can't leave you wandering about.'

He drags me down the corridor and throws me into the bedroom, then drags Mum and throws her onto the bed, she bounces, the pillow falls on the floor, Mouse falls out.

'What's this?' Lester picks up Mouse. 'This yours?'

I say nothing, which is never the thing to do. He doesn't hit me. He drags me back to the kitchen. Mouse goes on the table. He pulls out a knife from his bag of burglary tools.

'Your toy?' Lester taunts, before he chops Mouse into pieces. 'Not your toy now,' he says and rips the rest of Mouse to shreds.

I am dragged back to my room. He pushes me in.

'Just in case you change your mind about staying.' Lester closes the door and I hear the lock turn.

I'm still only just breathing when I hear his car leave. I couldn't save Mouse. I watched him chop her up. It was a challenge. With each chop he had stared, wanting to let me know that he could destroy any part of me. If I tried to stop him he would beat me, to prove one more time how useless I was. That I was his, his to hurt, and to make sure I knew there was absolutely nothing I could ever do to change that. There is no Mouse anymore.

o

Mum mutters. I can't make out what she says. If I touch her, she flinches and moans. Her leg is a mess. She doesn't really get dressed on days at home and she's wearing an old tunic top. So I can see the damage. At least the bleeding has stopped but it doesn't need an expert to know her right leg is broken. That means I need to get her to hospital or try.

She mumbles some more and now I can guess what she wants. The same as always. I see this as a chance to get her off the stuff. That's if we survive, which doesn't seem likely. If Lester isn't sending Mum to hospital, he probably isn't interested in whether she lives or dies.

There was something else going on in his mind. I don't want to know what it is, but I will find out soon enough and I'm sure it will be worse than bad. I think we are getting to the end. Mum is not going to do anything. It's up to me, either I do something, or I give up. Giving up would be so easy, just let it happen. But I am a different girl since finding the moor outside. I will not give up. I need to do something.

I pull the mattress from the bed onto the floor and roll and pull and push Mum onto it.

Mum's moaning is worse, frantic. I haven't got what she wants. But she did leave me some pills after Lester nearly killed me last time. They made me throw up, so I didn't take them all. I scrabble around for them, Mum is saying yes when I hold them in front of her. Lester didn't leave us any water, but Mum seems to be able to swallow them dry. Practice, I suppose. She's grabbed my arm. I guess she wants to keep me close for when she needs more. Doesn't look like I'm going to get her off her drug habit or anything. Are these pills the same stuff she injects? I need a chemist.

It takes ages, but Mum drifts off, her grip eases and I pull away. Now I reach for the tin which held the moor door key. I thought I might need other keys, and this is the time. They are all old and a bit rusty. I try them on the bedroom door. Success. The lock screeches and I'm telling it to be quiet. I did hear Lester's car leave but has he come back? Slowly I open the door and tiptoe down to the kitchen. No Lester.

I have to get out. To get help. The other doors are all locked. Even the door we came in is locked. There's only one broken pane of glass. I try all the keys, nothing fits. If I am going to get out, then I will have to smash a window. I think the one in the empty room down towards the front door will be easiest. I can use the poker. He's left it on the floor. I reach for it.

Noise. I hear the car pull into the garage. He's back. No time to escape. He'll find me, stop me and it will all be over. I have to get back to Mum and lock our door.

I turn to rush back. The cupboard by his mattress is slightly open. I can see the pile of papers. This is too risky. I hear the squeak of the garage door.

'Leave it, Molly,' I say to myself as I pull the cupboard door open and grab for as much paper as I can. 'Come on,' I almost scream at myself. I push the cupboard door shut, almost trip over the mattress. I hear his steps. No tiptoeing back, I run. The sound of his key in the door.

I dive into my room. I have to lock the door and I can't do this quietly. As I turn the lock I shout for help and bang the woodwork. Stepping back, I hide the key and the papers as I hear him coming.

The door opens.

'Stop that shouting,' he says. 'Shut it or you know what will happen.' He has the poker in his hand again and points it at Mum. She's still out of it.

'We have to get her to hospital,' I hear my small frightened voice.

He just sneers, closes and locks the door. I hear him in the kitchen, doing something. Sounds like he is carrying things from his car to the kitchen. It takes him ages. Mum mumbles for more pills. This time she can't swallow. I bang on the door again. There's an angry shout.

I shout back, that we need water. He swears at me and carries on banging about in the kitchen. I don't dare to look at the stuff from his cupboard in case he does appear, which happens a bit later.

He opens the door and pulls me out. 'Get down there and get what you need.' He pushes me towards the kitchen.

'Mum...' I'm still whining. 'Have to get help.' I turn to him. 'I'll do whatever you want, just help her.'

There is no trace of warmth in him. His face is set in an angry snarl which mixes with something worse that I think my suggestion has made him think about. It's a face I see when I have to be the good girl. Is he thinking about that even now? There is no end to this.

'Sure.' His breath is a little quicker. 'Sure, you'll do whatever I want. Just a quick one for now.' He shoves me forward.

I can't do this now. I won't do it. But Lester has looked at his watch. 'No time,' he growls to himself. 'Later.'

I'm given seconds to scrabble around for water and some scraps of food before he takes me back to our locked room. Too quickly to do much else, except look around the kitchen seeing what he has been doing. I can't make sense of it. He's brought in lamps on stands. Four of them. They are the sort of lights I've seen on the telly, lights they use for making films. I get an even worse feeling. I am shivering when the bedroom door is

117

locked again. I need help and there is no one to help. I sit on my mattress next to Mum. I pull my knees up to my chin and hold on. I'm still shivering, and the tears start. There is no way out of this.

Lester leaves again in the car. Mum is waving her arm around trying to grab for me. Her face is screwed up with pain. I give her the rest of the pills, and water, which she chokes on but still manages to swallow. She has hold of me again; it's a weaker hold now.

As Mum drifts away into snoring snuffling I move away. Have I got time to break out? If he comes back and catches me then I know it will get even worse. But I have to try.

Hopeless. Lester has left his key in the lock to our door, half-turned. I can't unlock it. I need something to poke his key out. I find a pencil. There were lots of pencils scattered on the floor from my throwing fit, and I had tidied them into a tin. The pencil doesn't work, I can't shift the key. There is no way I am able to clear the lock. Even if I did, he'd be able to see what I'd done. I'm back on the mattress.

This room always kept me in fear. The window high up on the wall gives light but has always made it feel like a prison. The smell of the moor on the old lady's coats didn't spread this far. The only thing I could smell was damp. Now it smells of me and Mum. Neither of us have been using the bathroom much. If anyone else came in here they'd probably say it stank. It's a brown, damp stinking room and I can't get out.

I jump up to the window and cling to the ledge. Can't hold on for long. Just enough to see there is no way out through here. I fall back to the mattress. Mum grunts but doesn't move. It's only when I've been sitting miserably for ages that I remember the papers I took from Lester's cupboard. I listen carefully; there is no sound, but I move to the door and listen again. No noise apart from the wind and creaking of the house. I still wait. I expect Lester to jump out from somewhere.

When I do start to check out what I've taken I do it one page at a time, keeping the rest hidden under a pillow. Not much of a hiding place and it makes me think of Mouse. This is too scary. It's not that I can't imagine what Lester will do if he finds I've pinched his stuff, it's because I can imagine exactly what he'll do, and knowing is much worse.

The first pages look like bills for water, electricity and things. They are all in the name of Mrs Penworthy – Doris Penworthy. The old lady's name. The mother of the woman I met with her map on the moor. I've often tried to imagine what Doris must have looked like. Has she died? There are letters in this pile that say something about a care home, about Doris going into a care home.

I don't think she has been paying her bills. The top one says they are going to take her to court if she doesn't pay. I don't know what the date is now, but this letter was sent in April and that has to be a few months ago. I flick through more bills and letters from people trying to sell stuff. None of it looks like things Lester would want to buy. Things for older people.

I find the certificates. One is a birth certificate for Doris, an ancient creased and faded paper. It's hard to read the year she was born in, looks like 1911. That would make her really old if she's still alive. Makes me think about the digging I saw in the garden when we arrived.

I hear a noise and stuff the papers away.

I wait to hear his footsteps outside the door. There's nothing. I've been holding my breath and I'm dizzy, with spots flashing in front of my eyes. It's all quiet. I suck in more air, but still listen. There are too many noises here in this house. I go back to hugging my knees and talking to Mum, who doesn't answer. Eventually I return to reading Lester's papers.

In the pile I took, there's a plastic envelope, looks different, newer. This looks like the thing Mum was interested in. She said we'd be all right when she saw it. We're never all right so I didn't take any notice of what she said. One is a certificate.

It's a certificate of marriage.

Lester's marriage to someone called Irene – Irene Penworthy. That could be Map Woman, so perhaps she didn't make up her name. Unless it's not her at all and she's pretending to be Irene.

The next is the "Last Will and Testament".

It says Doris leaves everything to her daughter Irene, it says ONLY in big red letters. ONLY to Irene for her safety and protection.

This fits with everything the woman said, the woman on the moor is Irene Penworthy. This house does belong to her and this must be the document she wanted me to find. Would it make any difference? If Irene had this could she throw Lester out? What happened to all of the stuff that must have been in this house? Lester must have sold it. I don't think that Irene, if that was the woman I met, I don't think she would manage to get Lester to do anything. Why had she married him? Why would anyone marry Lester?

I'm sort of ready for him when I hear the car again. It's getting late. I don't think whatever he's planning is going to happen today. Doesn't mean he'll leave me alone tonight. But he did say he needed to keep me looking pretty, so perhaps I may survive the night. I must find a way to get us out. I'll have to be an especially good girl if I want to do that. My thoughts are chasing all over the place. I know why. I'm trying not to go to one of them, to one thought that's trying to nag its way into my brain. It breaks through: what did Irene do to get that limp?

thirteen

I'm rocking backwards and forwards on this mattress. With each rock I try to think of something outside this room, outside this house. To take me away.

Rock – woolly horses. Map Woman said they were Dartmoor ponies. Who do they belong to? Irene said her mother used to take them food when it got cold and she meant when the snow covered the moor, covered the ground outside this house. I'm back here in the room again.

Rock – the post box, Cranmere Pool. I see the soldiers. I want to feel good about them, but they left, everybody leaves except me. Stay here and I'm back in this room with my smashed-up mum.

Rock – it's no use. Every thought goes wrong. I can't escape. My head is full of pokers and that man. What is he doing in the kitchen? Those lights. I really do not want to think about them, but I can't stop. I have the worst feeling.

The key turns in the lock. Lester, with poker in hand, shoves the door open and calls for me. No more thinking.

Lester is looking me over. I am a mess. I still have on the

clothes I found for walking. My hair is matted with sweat and dirt. Lester doesn't like what he sees.

'Got to get you cleaned up.' He frowns. Looking at Lester I'm not sure he knows how to do cleaning up, but I can see he's thinking about it – slowly. And he looks confused.

'Mum,' I say.

'Eh?'

'You've got to get Mum to hospital.' I point at her bloodied leg. 'She'll die if you don't.'

Again, I can see him churning over his thoughts. Whatever Lester is planning I think he's out of his depth. He looks worried, jumpy, still confused. If I push him, he'll turn to violence. I have to help him if I want to get out of this mess. Hard to help him but I must do it.

'If you get Mum to hospital it'll be much easier,' I choke. 'Much easier for me to be your good girl.' Saying those words hurts so badly. Almost worse than it happening to me. I have given in. I am swapping myself to get something.

Nat said it was the only way. 'If you want something you've got to give something and the only thing you've got to give is yourself.'

I have time to go over those thoughts because Lester is still frowning, rubbing his head, looking backwards and forwards. I finally realise that he is very stupid.

'You know that's a good idea.' I think he'll want to feel this comes from him.

I see him nod his head. 'Yep. I was going to do that.'

Lester steps forward and picks Mum up in his arms. He isn't gentle. I think the pain will make her scream but she's pretty much unconscious. She only wails when her leg bangs against the door as Lester carries her out. I follow.

'Get back,' he shouts at me.

'I need to come.' I shouldn't have said that. I have gone too far. His face reddens, the snarl appearing. I think he's going to drop Mum and turn on me.

I move back. 'Sorry, sorry,' I say in my pathetic voice. 'Just take her, please.'

Lester struggles with the door, with the key, with Mum. He's back to lock me in. I hear them leave. For a while I feel I have won a battle and if I can do that then…

The "while" isn't very long. Nat's words are still there – it's the only way. I don't have anything to give that Lester doesn't take anyway.

o

I am left alone for another day, locked in this room alone. I have drunk the water, but I don't eat. Without Mum the room echoes with emptiness. Not much light comes in through the window. It's pointing the wrong way. Lester comes and goes. He doesn't answer when I scream questions about Mum.

On the next day, with Lester out again and as the evening sun is fading, I look up at the grimy panes of glass. A face. I shriek before I recognise Irene, Map Woman. She must have climbed up and she's tapping on the glass and waving at me and saying something. The way she does it worries me, tight screwed-up lines on her forehead and she keeps looking over her shoulder. It makes me think about her limp.

She says something, too quiet for me to hear.

She says it again, 'Have you got it?' I just hear her call in a mix of whisper and shout. 'Quick.' She waves again, more frantically this time.

I do have something, and I know it is what she wants. I start forward to get the Last Will and Testament. Under the pillow. I have got it for her. Stop, Mol. Is Irene going to get you out of here? She's strange and I don't feel I can trust her. But it's hard to resist when she's going berserk outside the window.

'Let me out.' My voice is a shout.

'Shsss,' she almost cries. 'Have you got it?'

I don't trust her, and I think if I say no then she will just go.

'Yes.' I mimic her loud whisper. 'Come and get me out.'

Her face disappears. I get the paper. I hear the door open into the kitchen. She must have a key. Again, I wonder why Irene didn't just get in and find the will by herself. Why did she need me? Now she's at my door, scrabbling with this lock. She comes in.

'Give it to me,' Irene says, and her whole body is shaking. She can hardly stand. She must know what Lester can do, what he does, what he has done to her.

'Let's get out.' I push against her, but she doesn't move. I stop. We are both frozen.

The car is back.

Irene grabs the will from me. She's out of the door. The lock turns. I hear her go further back along the corridor. Lester is in the kitchen. There is no way out for Irene. Can she hide?

I am alone again. Irene has what she wants. I don't think she can help me now that Lester is back. She's too scared. If he finds her, I think he might kill her. Why did they get married? I think Lester only wants young girls, she's too old. She must have had something but why would she have agreed to marry him – why would anyone with any sense do that? There has to be a lot more she hasn't told me. Or is she just completely crazy?

Lester doesn't come back to me yet. He's doing something.

I hear him moving in the kitchen, noises in the bathroom, taps running, more stuff being dragged around. He whistles. Maybe he thinks he's being brave, but the whistling sounds ragged. What is going to happen? Can it be worse? Is there anything that can be worse than what has already happened? I don't need Nat's words to tell me there is something worse.

I'm worried that he wasn't gone very long when he took Mum, was it long enough to get to a hospital? I want to ask him what happened. But he doesn't come back to me for ages.

When he does, he enters the room with, 'Run you a nice bath,' and I hear anxiety in his voice.

'Mum?' I cry. 'How is she? What happened?'

That gets me another smack. 'Don't ask me about that slag. I fixed her fine.'

I try again.

'If you ask one more time, I don't care – you get the poker.' He pauses. 'After you've got my money back of course.' He hits me again around the head.

Lester grabs me by the arm and drags me through the kitchen. I don't ask about Mum again. Things I don't want to know. Lester pulls me into the room I found before. The one with the plant crashing against the window. It's still crashing but the room isn't empty anymore. The lights are positioned around the room at each corner. Then in front of the sooty fireplace is a giant camera. That's not all.

He must have dragged the mattress down from Mum's room. And of all the weird ideas he's tried to decorate the room, as though it would be mine. With pictures of things that little girls might have. All in pink. Nothing can make this empty space real. Not even the unlit candles, I can already smell their scent of something sweet and sickly.

'Like it?'

I think he really is expecting me to say yes.

'Why?' I say instead. He doesn't have an answer. The room is a film set. He sees the terror on my face and that seems to give him back the confidence.

'For the party,' he sneers. 'Got to get you ready for the party. For the rest of them. Soon get my money back.' I'm dragged into the bathroom.

I am snivelling, tears and snot. I have not won any battles. He pulls me into the bathroom.

Even the moor cannot take me away. My hate is too strong. The forever hate is too strong. I want to do very bad things to this man. I want him dead.

I am washed.

And when I cry for help, I am pushed under the water. And when I surface, I hear the slightest sound of a door closing. Lester is enjoying himself too much to hear Irene escaping with the only thing I had. The will was the only thing she wanted. I didn't rate in her plans.

I am dressed. It's new, it's pink and disgusting. I have a handbag, also pink. Stupid shoes. Something red on my lips, he's thought this out. My mind has shut down. Lester tells me the others will be here soon. I know he means other men. Men like Lester. He's found a way to get his money back. I am going to get the money for him.

He takes me back to the locked bedroom. 'I'll bring you out when they are all here, nice surprise. A good girl for them all.'

I wonder why Lester tells me this. Is it to make it worse for me, to hurt me, knowing what will happen? I feel there is something more, something that makes him worry about what will happen. If Lester has set something up that he can't control, then will either of us be alive at the end of his "party"? I don't think so. Perhaps that is for the best. At least I will not have to think about it when I'm dead.

I look around the room, wondering if there is anything that could help me escape. Nothing. Even if I could smash the window, which I can't because I don't have anything to do that with, but even if I could, Lester would hear the noise. I have nothing.

I hear more cars. They must have parked in the lane. Voices. Rough male voices. I think I hear the garage man. Has he just come to take what is owed to him or is he going to join in the party? My stomach heaves and I retch but I've had no food to throw up.

I hear the laughs. Bottles being opened.

Then Lester is back at my door. He waves to me to follow him, doesn't grab me. It's a different look, a little scared. It's almost as though he wants to believe we are in this together. For me to be his friend. Perhaps he doesn't know the men who are drinking in the kitchen. I give him my coldest stare and I think he flinches. But probably not. A cold stare from a little girl in a foul fluffy pink dress could never work. It's just that Lester is even more pathetic. That gives me just a tiny bit of hope. I have a small idea. Two, actually. And I don't care if they don't work. Nothing can make this worse than it is.

fourteen

I walk ahead, Lester pushing me on into the gloomy kitchen. The lamp isn't on, candles have been lit in here. It's dark and smoky with cigarettes. There's music. I don't know what it is, something with a thumping base.

Garage Man is in charge here. He's sitting at one side but seems to take up the whole room. Across from him are five pigs. Not real piggy pigs. They are men disguised with pig masks. There are glasses and bottles, several empty.

With my head hung, I notice their shoes. Slip-on shoes. No use for walking on the moor, I think. Easy to take off. I move that thought away from my head.

I get a look at Garage Man's face. In a horror movie he wouldn't need make-up. And I think we are headed for something like that.

'Hello Molly.' He speaks and my legs give way. He leans over and picks me up by the neck of this awful dress and holds me above the ground. 'Have to thank Bill for arranging this evening.'

Bill? Who is Bill? It's Lester who nods. It's only me that has a real name. The pigs have no names or faces. Now I know I am not leaving here alive.

The way Garage thanks him makes me think that Bill is not his best friend. Makes me think that Garage isn't into this, just the money which I don't think will save me.

They've been running an auction. For the film, Lester/Bill tells them. Also for the order in which they will "entertain" me in the candle-lit room Lester has set up. They can't say any words that sound like what they really want to do, that would be too disgusting. Lester is talking. I am trying so hard not to listen as he explains about the filming. It's easier when I turn to look at Garage. He has disgust on his face.

The auction is going well for them. The drink is going well too. When I am put back on the floor I still cannot stand, and I am left to sit as they take shifty looks at me and offer more money. There's a pile of it on the table.

'Smile, Molly.' Lester/Bill is trying to push up the price.

I am Molly who walks on Dartmoor. I have climbed the Tors. I have run across bogs. What is happening here cannot be real. They are not real people. They are pigs. I am the only real person here. I have my plan. I will get my voice.

Garage is very still. He is more frightening when he is silent. He doesn't frighten me in the way Lester does. There is something far more serious about Garage. I can see that Lester feels it. He's clumsy like I am when I am out of my mind with fear.

Garage speaks.

'Bill, why do you get all scaredy outside on the moor?'

Thump, thump, goes the music or is it my heart. The five men seem to stop with their glasses halfway to their open mouths.

Only Garage Man looks up in this frozen room. 'It was your wife who told me about you and the moor.' Garage is taunting. 'She doesn't like you very much, does she?'

This will be my revenge for Mouse. No matter what is going to happen I will join in, for Mouse.

'He does,' I say my bit. 'Wets himself out on the moor.' I have no idea where this came from. It is far more likely that I am going to be the one wetting myself. But I think Mum might have told me some of this. I didn't listen to her much, but she had been mumbling something about Lester and the moor.

'Rubbish… rubbish,' Lester/Bill blusters. 'She's making it up, aren't you? Tell Carl it isn't true.' Lester is talking to me. He's not smashing his fist into me, not kicking me, he's asking me. In fact, I think he's actually pleading.

The garage man isn't called Carl here tonight. He's meant to be called Tommy or something else which sounds so much friendlier than he looks, and right now his face is pumped forward, teeth bared as though he is about to strike.

Lester is shaking.

Tommy/Carl/Garage Man says very slowly, 'You shouldn't have called me that.'

I shiver at his words. They sound like a death sentence, although I can't see why he thinks he can hide behind a false name. There can't be many people that large, working in a garage near here. But I don't mind that. I think Garage was looking for an excuse and Lester has given it to him.

'Sorry, sorry, she made me…' Lester squirms. It feels there is no way out of this for him.

'So, he gets all scared, does he?' I think Garage is trying to smile; it's not a friendly look. And he's talking to me, which should make me start to shake as well, but I am too far into this.

Molly will not shake.

'He goes all weak and floppy, like one of those bunnies out

there.' I really must have made that up – any rabbits on the moor are not floppy at all.

'Lester the flopsy bunny.' It's a Garage laugh.

'I'm… Bbbob… aren't I called Bob?' Lester gabbles.

'Not anymore, you're flopsy bunny now and you're going for a hop out there.' No one would argue with anything Garage says.

'Can't. It's agora-whatsit, I've got the agora thing, can't go outside,' Bill weeps.

The fuse on a firework has been lit. I should be scared. We are all going to die in here. Everyone except Garage. Not so much a firework, more a bomb.

'I want to see what flopsy bunny does.' Garage looks at the men. 'Don't you?'

The five men nod like toy dogs on the back shelf of a car. Well, toy pigs anyway. They aren't together. I have a feeling they would kill each other if Garage wants that to happen. They keep on with their nervous nodding.

'Don't do it. Please. I'll get your money back, anything,' Lester squeals, and falls to his knees.

'Of course you will,' Garage's pretend sympathy sounds like madness.

The men are in a competition to side with Garage. He laughs, they laugh.

Now Lester has his turn to get lifted up. Garage has him by the throat. 'Call this payment,' he sneers. 'Come on, Molly, let's see what he does outside.'

I don't really believe it but now I have to go on. I have a plan. I never thought I would get to use it. Now I shake with fear; I don't think I will be able to do it, have to try. This is a new world for Molly.

'Need a wee,' I gurgle and without asking run for the bathroom. One of the men makes a move as though he might follow me, but Garage tells him he has to wait until after the auction. The other pigs nod to that.

I'm into the bathroom. Keep the door open. Count to ten. Run to the camera room. Overturn the lighted candles onto the bed. The fire takes immediately. I shut the door. Back to the loo. Flush. Run out. Lester is being dragged towards the door to the moor. They are all in the corridor. Garage has pushed the pig mask men forward. He turns back to me. Does he know what I've done? I think he's coming back to tear me apart. That's what his face seems to say. But it's not what he does.

'GET THE MONEY,' he mouths without sound before he pushes the others towards the moor door.

I know it's locked. They will come back, and my plan won't work. Garage isn't interested in keys. The door comes off with the frame as he kicks it out. The noise is a distraction and gives me time to sweep the pile of cash into my stupid pink handbag. Then I run after them. There's smoke already coming under the door to the room the men want to take me to.

Lester is screaming. This is Garage's fun. Frightening people and he loves frightening Lester. I almost feel sorry for him – not. Lester is weeping and pleading. Garage says he's worse than me. 'A great big girl.'

There's just enough light out here. The tors stand out against a deep purple sky. Looking back, I think there's going to be a lot more light soon, from the burning house. Garage makes the men follow him. I wouldn't miss this. Lester's forever is looking worse than mine. Garage throws him on the ground.

Lester's screaming, 'Help me,' and trying to grab hold of

Garage's legs, to pull himself up the body of this huge man as though holding on will save him.

'Come on, Lester, give us a hop, now you're a bunny.' Garage kicks him away. It's a hard kick and Lester is almost thrown into the air. 'Good one, try it yourself. Hop.'

Lester falls apart. He's trying to hop. He's howling. He's wet himself. Whatever this agora thing is, it's killing him.

Garage is really into this. He kicks Lester again. Much more of this and Lester is dead. Do I want him to die? That was the forever I came here with, forever hating forever wishing death to Lesters. Can I get over that? Can I change forever?

'Stop, stop.' I run to Garage, pull him off, save Lester. Except I don't, and I don't have to.

The fire in the house explodes. The roof cracks open with the noise of a real bomb. Flames leap out. Slates spew into the air like a display.

'Christ,' Garage shouts, and it sounds as though he finds it funny. He certainly looks in my direction and points with his fingers in the shape of a pretend gun.

Lester doesn't see it. He's buried himself into wet moorland bog. His wailing is still loud enough to be heard.

The five men don't look at each other. They're off, sprinting for their cars, still trying to hold their masks on. Garage doesn't run. He turns to me with his hand outstretched. I give him the pink handbag. It would look strange in his massive hand if this night had been something normal. Nothing can look strange after this.

Garage reaches out again, and I think that this is time for me to die. He ruffles my hair; it must be what all dangerous men do. 'Best you leg it, too.'

On Dartmoor in a pink dress with pink heeled shoes?

Garage shrugs. Lester moans. Garage gives him a mighty kick and there is no more noise. He leaves and I make for the bushes. The flames have lit the sky. It seems an age before I hear sirens coming. I crouch down and wait. I am alone on my moor.

Not quite.

Irene is coming. She's seen me. She strides over. 'Why did you have to burn my house?' She slaps me round the head.

Irene has not realised that I am a very different Molly tonight. I kick and scream and bite and punch and pull at her hair which comes away in chunks. She tries to run. I'm after her, leaping on her back, pulling her to the ground. I am still attacking her when the first of the rescue men arrive and pull me off.

fifteen

The social is not quite what I expect. Even the word "social" is out of date, an old term, something from my gran's time. Not sure what it's called now. Doesn't really matter because whatever it is, I am right in it.

It started with, 'What on earth are you doing out here – dressed like that?' Words from a fireman as he pulled me off Irene.

I say nothing. Every bit of me has given way and I collapse onto the dark wet ground. The fireman leaves me there with Irene, who he must think is my mum. The fireman leaves us because he has rather a lot to do, with hoses, more fire engines arriving, men in spaceman gear, radios blaring static into the Dartmoor night. It's quite warm, what with there being a big fire not far away.

Irene is having some full-on raging anger stomp, shouting, 'Why?' and swearing at me. I don't have enough in me to do anything about it, even though I want to. It all feels a bit blurry. The fire still spits huge lumps of sparking stuff into the air. It's like watching a film or something, not real. More people seem to be arriving all the time.

The gate to the moor has been opened, letting in vehicles. I heard the snap of the bolt cutters breaking through the chain. Floodlights are being set up. Makes me think back to the room in the house, with the camera. That felt real. Makes me puke and I retch; with not much in my stomach it's just something nasty and yellow that spills over my pink outfit. No one takes any notice. Some of me feels I must be okay with all this going on, I don't have to go with the pigs, aren't I saved? Doesn't feel like that.

'Mum!' I call out loud in some useless cry. There never has been a mum.

No one hears. Irene is still ranting, sometimes at me. Should I have run off as Garage told me? Where to? I'm not going looking for strangers, the damp moor grass feels much safer than people, although I do wish my African soldiers were here.

An ambulance with siren and hooting noises splitting the air comes through the gate, slowly pulling onto the grass. Two women in green uniform jump out.

'Over there,' points one of the firemen, who must be in charge. A woman fireman. My mind is churning in bizarre wheels, are women firemen called firewomen? Are they called something else completely different? I almost get up to ask them, it seems so important to me.

They go to Lester. Is he dead? They're calling for more light, and one of the floodlights is turned on Lester who is stretched out, half in a prickly bush, and not moving. One of the ambulance women runs back to the ambulance and gets a huge bag. Whatever they're doing looks like they're poking him about. The light beam is picking out smoke, so this is weird and hazy. It's getting warmer, I think the wind has changed.

Someone is barking into a radio; I hear the word helicopter. That must mean Lester isn't dead, surely. Do I want him to die? I thought that last kick from Garage had done it. Now I don't feel anything.

Another ambulance is coming. I can see blue lights flashing from down the road. Someone comes over to me, shines a torch in my face. I'd forgotten about the lipstick Lester had smeared on me after that bath. I guess with the puking and wiping my face I must look – actually I probably fit in with this whole scene quite well.

Men jump out of the ambulance.

'Is your mum around?' one of them asks.

Irene has vanished. Can't even hear her ranting.

'What mum?' I say in a confused way.

That doesn't really work. It's not an answer that meets with their approval.

They start to poke me, I suppose that means check me over, but I start to feel it's Lester again and I'm screaming and kicking again, rather weakly this time.

'Confused,' one of them says very definitely, before turning to me. 'Did you hit your head, love?'

I stop kicking. I start to laugh. I can't stop. It's not real laughter, some wild and scary noise I make. And I don't stop. Why is hitting my head so funny? Don't they mean has someone hit you on the head? One of them picks me up and I'm carried down the road to the second ambulance. I feel I'm leaving a war film and carry on giggling now, in bursts.

Behind me the firemen are moving everyone to a different bit of the moor because of the wind and sparks. Everyone from the village, which isn't many, have gathered to watch. They are being told to move away. I hear the sound of the helicopter. I hear the voices of the village people. They sound so far away, getting even further, further. I can't feel my legs, my arms, my head. Then nothing.

o

I am on a hard bed, a bed with bars at the side, it's a cot. I don't like the bars. I hit my hand against the metal. I sit up. My head isn't great, even though I didn't hit it. I look around. This has to be a hospital, all white walls and a green curtain pulled around my bed. Not a bed, it's a trolley. I can hear voices. I am not wearing my pink dress; they have put me in a gown thing with ribbons tied at the back. I am ashamed. They have seen my body. I need to get out of here.

If this is a hospital maybe Mum is here, maybe I can find her. I crawl quietly down to the end of the trolley to escape. The gown pulls up around me. I need my walking gear. That thought is like having a bucket of water thrown over me. I'm shivering. I can't get out, they'll stop me. The voices are nearer now. I give a moan.

Whisssh. The curtain pulls back. I see the nurse. I know when I see her face that she has decided everything about me.

She calls back over her shoulder, 'The poor thing has come round.'

Another nurse arrives to see the "poor thing". I am the poor thing. I lie down and turn my head away from them. I DO NOT WANT TO BE A POOR THING. That's part of forever. Nat told me about poor thing people. It happened after the social got you. You became a poor thing. Nat explained how a poor thing was almost as bad as being a good girl. Poor things still got pain.

The nurses are tutting. 'Does it hurt?' One of them goes round to the other side of the trolley. There is no escape from them. She pulls down the front of my gown. The cigarette burn hasn't healed well and still oozes. I snatch the gown back.

'Must hurt dreadfully,' she says, in a voice that tells me I am both a poor thing and a victim. She pulls the gown down again for a closer look; victims aren't allowed to be in control. 'Who could have done such a thing?' She isn't asking me a question. Her face has screwed as though she wants me to know how angry she is about the burn. She doesn't want anything from me, such as a full description of what happened, she doesn't want anything from me other than to be a good girl – just a different type.

I don't want to give her an explanation either. I want to shut it from my mind, like I have done before. On this trolley, in this hospital, I can't seem to bring the moor back. Can't see it, can't smell it, can't use it to take me away from cigarette burns.

'Found out her name yet?' A man peers round the curtain. He must be a doctor. They've run out of women.

'Look at this.' The nurse is trying to show him the burn.

'Awful,' he says. 'Don't think anything is broken.'

How does he know? Of course, he has looked me over after I passed out or whatever happened to me. Did they give me something to make that happen? For all I know this doctor puts on a pig mask at night and goes out for entertainment. I lean over and check his shoes. Black lace-ups, but he could have changed.

They have been asking me questions. I have missed them, too concerned about pigs. They want my name. Why don't you give me a mask, and I will make up names even if it's obvious

I'm not being truthful? At first, they continue with their smiley faces and drippy voices but when I don't answer in the way they want, it turns to something different and harder.

'Because poor things are to blame for being poor things,' Nat had said. Actually, lying here, I realise that it wasn't Nat who said that. It wasn't actually Nat who said all the things I imagined. She'd be talking to us in the big room we shared and one of the women would come back and take up the words. It wasn't Nat who talked about blame. It was a woman, and I guess she was quite young really and got all tearful about blame and how everyone thought it was her fault.

'Molly,' I give them to stop the questions.

'The police surgeon will be along in a moment.' The doctor moves off.

Now I am back with terror and nothing to protect me. Nothing I can bring into my head. Worse, this gown I'm wearing reminds me of those horror movies when they take the screaming girl off to be chopped up. We watched a lot of those – age certificates didn't count. And I do know that surgeons cut people up. Why is a surgeon coming soon, and a police one? They are going to cut me up like the movie.

I'm off, down the end of the bed, onto the floor, brush past a nurse, barge past the doctor who is saying something like 'look here' in a posh voice and I'm in a corridor, glass door at the end, they're after me but I am quick – quick as a girl who instead of the moor has a movie picture of a graveyard on a stormy night and a lot of blood. Through the door. I'm in a car park. I stop. Lots of people. Men with cameras pointed at me. Flashing lights. I curl up on the ground, I must hide. All I can see are men with slip-on shoes. It is the police surgeon who leads me back into the hospital and he isn't going to cut me up.

The police surgeon is about eight foot tall. Slowly I find out that the hospital is a very small one in the little town we came to on the bus. Perhaps I should have guessed that because it's still raining a bit. He tells me his name is Sam. Inspector Sam and he knows what he is doing and for the first time I feel better. A tiny bit of me wonders if he is related to Garage, because of his size. Also, because I am starting to invent that Garage was actually the shining armour knight I'd been wanting.

'Can I call you Molly?' Sam asks me, after he's got me back on my trolley bed. He actually seems to want me to make a decision like a real person. I nod but I'm still pulling at the gown to cover as much of me as possible.

He explains. Tells me that there are probably awful things that people will ask me about. 'But not now.' He's quite at home in this hospital and they do what he asks. My clothes, like the pink dress, have been taken away for examination. I know what that is, I've seen the crime TV and I know about forensics, this is getting more interesting. He says I need clothes that are more comfortable, but he says that none of this is going to be easy, and asks me if there is anything I need to tell him, right now.

I think. I worry. He has a look that makes me want to tell him things but even the new brave Molly is too frightened.

'You are safe now, Molly,' he says it slowly, and perhaps I can believe him. He's not wearing a uniform. I don't need to check his shoes, because he's much too big to have been one of the pig men.

'Mum,' I mutter, and I see him smile. I can see he feels he has won this small victory and although that scares me again, I like his smile. But it doesn't last for long.

I tell him about Mum and her broken leg and how she

was taken to hospital which might have been yesterday. Her name doesn't seem to be recognised. I hope that means she's gone to a different hospital. It doesn't. I give Inspector Sam a description of Mum. It's not a very good description but he nods. He knows.

'Molly.' He takes a deep breath. 'Molly, did your mother take drugs?'

My open mouth is enough of an answer. The smile has gone completely. The questions stop. He explains that he has to make sure about something. How we have to leave the hospital and go down to his police station. I don't ask for any more. There are so many things I don't want to know, and this is just another. Lester wasn't away for long. Lester didn't take Mum to hospital. Inspector Sam didn't ask if Mum takes drugs, just if she used to. Mum hasn't given up drugs since yesterday. She has injection marks all over her. Injection marks and a broken leg. I don't need to ask what he knows. I bury myself into the pillow. I'm not crying. I just want to see nothing.

o

They consider me too young to be able to hear, so they talk about secret things in loud whispers.

Inspector Sam is replaced by others. We don't go to his police station for long. I am driven away to a bigger town with a bigger building and while the people aren't actually bigger in size, they are more important. And the word I couldn't have heard them whisper is 'murder'.

o

143

By the time I get taken to an ordinary white house, with a family and two children and a dog, cat, goldfish, hamster and a garden with a swing, I have been talked at by many people. I have heard explanations for why things have to be done, why other things are not going to be done and what things may or may not happen. As these go on it is obvious to me that what is not going to be done and what may not happen are the things that I want to happen and know about. They are the things that I am not old enough to talk about or do.

What I know I should be doing, because I have seen so many doing it on the telly, is being taken to a place where bodies are stored in racks. Then they pull out one sheet-covered body and the sheet is pulled back and they ask me if it is my mum. I know I should be doing this because I don't think there are any other relatives alive to do the identification, dental records are non-existent, medical records were not in her real name nor was her driving licence and she has no passport. If I didn't know all that, I work it out in chats with the important people. It is considered too awful for me to have to go to a mortuary and see the murdered body of my mum. I could say I have seen a lot worse. They do it with DNA swabs.

In corridors outside of wherever I am I hear, 'Can't believe it, her mum, did that, sold her.'

There are obviously a lot of people who can't believe it. That's not surprising, I think, because I can't either. Didn't really believe it at the time. Not sure how I should feel. I loved the mum I wanted, only occasionally the one I got. I'm more angry because her death feels like my fault. I made Lester take her. I should have known he wouldn't take her to hospital. Why would he? Too many questions.

The other thing that may not happen which I would

quite like to take place is a trial of Lester for a whole range of awfulness. Might not happen because he's in intensive care. I will have to wait and see.

I didn't have to wait for the stuff that has to be done and is going to happen whether I like it or not. I know all that will stick in my mind. But not for now.

o

I am expected to settle into my new foster home.

'Come in,' Mrs New Foster Mum says. Not said, but heavily in her words, are 'poor thing'.

I meet the two children and a dog, the cat, the goldfish, the hamster and I am taken to see the swing which I can play on anytime I want. I doubt she means the middle of the night which I think is most likely the time I will wish to use it – I doubt I am going to sleep unless I have a gun under my pillow.

And the bathroom. Which I need to spend a month in, washing away anything that can be washed away. Except my hair. Makes me think of Mum and that should be a good thought, us together, her brushing my hair. It's not. She brushed it for Lester. I want it cut off.

The house is very white and covered in pebbly stuff. There is a man. The children call him Dad. I am told I can call him Sydney or Dad if I like. I have to hold on to something after they say that. If they had said "daddy" I would have left sooner, faster and possibly with more damage than is going to happen later, although that would be difficult.

They know about me.

They all know about me.

Now what do you think two teenage boys will do with that

knowledge? To the poor thing that has arrived in their house? They have had other foster children, they've met other poor things but none quite as interesting as me. I am more thing than poor although not in terms of money. They want me to tell them about it. They want to talk late into the night when their parents can't hear. They are much more straightforward than the counsellors I have seen and will see again. They don't beat around any bushes. They want to know who did what and what got stuck in where, and with their questions they are having to hold something on their laps because, for them, it is too exciting.

I don't talk.

Now what do you expect two excited teenage boys do with the non-talking poor thing? They torment me. No violence because the police have told them my body is evidence and needs looking after. No unexplained bruises can happen to me. They torment me with poor thing words. And they tell me what they think happened, what Lester did. All very accurate, do they have a manual?

o

Over a few days I am taken to places. The house is in a town. They did tell me where; I don't have a map and I'm not asking for anything because I do not want to owe these people. Apart from the tormenting, the fosterers do try. My foster mum poor things me around the shops – I need clothes – and I am poor thinged around parks and walking the dog. I get my hair cut, short. Shaved would be better but not allowed. Mrs Foster Mum looks at me as though I am a broken princess, and it makes me feel like dog shit. I am starting to boil. My forever is starting to boil, and I have no way out.

Day three I am taken to see another doctor or two. I get examined, again. When they touch me, I flinch because I am waiting for the blows. There are no blows or grunting. It's cold and smells of disinfectant. They say how sorry they are while they turn me over. Pictures are taken. I think they are the sort of photos Lester and the pig men would have taken as souvenirs. Nat hadn't told me about the hospital stuff. I can't switch it off while they do it and that really gets to me. There is breakable stuff in this room, I break it. They say more sorrys, but tell me it has to be done, for the trial of Lester, if it happens. I am not persuaded. After a lot of whispers, I am given something to drink. I am not shown the pictures.

I don't want to hurt the foster mum. Hurting her is so stuck in the bad forever that I should not do it. I can't work out how to get rid of anything. I hate and hate and hate. I have no compass to get me out of it. I don't even want to hurt the boys. Or the dog and things. Not even Sydney, who wears slip-on shoes but hasn't pushed into the bathroom unexpectedly or come into my bedroom at night or done anything that I would expect as normal. I don't want to do it, but I do.

I only know one way out. I found the petrol in the garage.

It's a treble hit. Police, fire and ambulance arrive. Actually, a four thingy, because my care worker turns up. Poor things have to have a care worker. She looks fed up, tuts a lot and uses her phone. We're outside because the white pebble house isn't safe anymore.

The family, holding the animals, are staring at me with death threat eyes but not swearing because I am still a poor thing, even if I have reduced their house to smouldering rubble.

Should I say I am sorry? That is not a skill I have learnt; being really sorry hasn't featured in my life. This hasn't made me feel any better, but I am pretty sure it will happen again.

The next stop is somewhere called a secure unit. Here the dogs are all outside. No sign of a goldfish or hamster. This is more my sort of place. It's filled with damaged people. Other girls break enough things to make me feel calm, other girls try to burn the place down, it is enough. I am at home... for a while.

sixteen

It's a different sort of chaos that I am in now. Days can go by with nothing happening, except perhaps a fight in the secure unit, and there's always screaming. Over several days different people come to see me.

Today my care worker comes first. She's new. Other girls here have big heavy care workers and call them scare workers, but I'm not here for the same sort of thing. So, my care workers aren't scary or heavy, they wear cardigans that could have been knitted by their grans, assuming their grans weren't like mine. She asks me questions as though I'm ill.

'Hello Molly, are you better today? Did you sleep alright? How are you getting on with the other girls?'

I think slowly. Better than what? Don't know. Sleep? Difficult with the screaming. Other girls? I stay away from them; you should see what they do to each other given the chance. I'm a new poor thing and I think that's going to give me perhaps one more day before I become an easy target. Glad I did all that walking on the moor. You need to be fit in here.

Cardy-care worker isn't really wanting answers. She's just

talking, and I think she's terrified of this place. Possibly terrified of me! Whoopee!

We are joined by a large lady wearing an overtight suit and carrying a case that looks cheap. I am obviously an idiot who cannot understand anything, or that's the way they talk to me.

'This man (I guess they mean Lester) has done some very bad things, and needs to be punished,' says Cheap Case.

Punished? What do I take that to mean? In my head I am imagining torture. There was stuff on the telly about tying people down on a board and pouring water on them like they were drowning. That's fine by me for Lester.

'So, there's going to have to be a big meeting when important people decide what should happen.'

This is not clear. What is this woman talking about? Hasn't she watched *CSI*? Or even afternoons with *Murder She Wrote* or really old black and white ones when you're desperate? Doesn't she know there has to be a trial in a courtroom with wiggy people and shouting and an old man banging his hammer and calling 'SILENCE' and saying he'll clear the court? Does she know nothing? If she's part of this then Lester will get off. I've stopped listening.

I am lucky. Along with these two ladies, one of the secure unit staff has stayed in the room. Becky's nice in a 'you do that and you're dead' sort of way. She wears rubber-soled shoes, clothes that would stop me stabbing her to death and a huge bunch of keys. I see her looking at the other two and I guess she's thinking these bozos wouldn't last five minutes in this unit. She's here to make sure I don't kill them. Which, with my developing history, is clearly a possibility.

When Cheap Case and Cardy leave I am waiting for Becky to take me back to the day room.

'What was that about?' I ask her, and she rolls her eyes, and we walk out.

'Your pervert man (and she really does mean Lester) is out of hospital but this lot say he's too sick to remember anything. That's crap and he'd go to jail, but they aren't sure you'd make a good witness.'

'Why didn't they tell me that?'

'They did, but it was all in a mix with teddy bears and other cuddly toys so you wouldn't be scared,' she laughs. 'They don't know you and they didn't notice you'd gone to sleep.'

I'm left in the day room. I get stares and whispers. But I need to think. I am still not all in my bad forever world. Becky talks to me like I have arrived at that place. Like I am one of the team, her and me, the ones that understand the bad things. The ones that don't believe anything good will come of anything.

Oh shit, the other girls have come for me. I'm not getting another easy day. I will not cry. The girls want my story. They are more persuasive than the pebble-house teenagers. Shanna leads the pack from the yellow corner. She would give any cage fighter a hard time (cage fighting – one of the women in London left us with a DVD of how to do it). I tell them. They aren't hitting me, yet.

I talk.

Shanna shrugs. 'Call that bad?'

I do cry, it seems safest.

'Pussy,' Shanna puffs and walks away, but after a few steps, when her troop aren't watching, she turns and gives me a nod. My story was bad enough to be okay. So long as Shanna protects me, I may get a few more easy days. May. But Shanna's nod washed over me like some sort of warm blanket. Through that look I saw Dartmoor again, wild and wet but mine.

I don't need more easy days here because I get moved. I'm not meant to be in a secure unit because I haven't done anything – well, if you ignore the damage – but most of the other girls have been to court after doing some crime or other. I'm meant to be a poor thing who is the victim. Not sure which is worse. But it means they are meant to find me foster homes rather than prisons. So, it's more pebble-dashed houses. They put me in places without other children. I don't wreck the houses and I don't stay in one place for long. The foster people in these homes are specialists in difficult children. If I had done more damage, I would be "difficult" so I'd probably stay longer. Moving on is a bit like the time me and Mum had after we left Gran. People were after us then. Now they've caught me.

The people who talk to me like I'm an idiot won't tell me much about Mum. I ask questions and get stupid answers. Eventually I find out it is because of the trial. Apparently, I'll find out all about it then. Mum keeps me awake at night. I want her and I don't. Not knowing what happened means I invent what happened and that keeps me awake, because it's down to Lester. I guess he dumped her. It's what he did next that keeps me awake.

Cardy follows me from home to home. I suppose she'll stay with me until I do lose it again, which is getting closer. I get more visits from Cheap Case woman. They've told me their names. I forget on purpose. They sort of ask me questions about what happened, what I remember, what it was like in Lester's house. I don't think they believe I will make a good witness. I'm sure I'd do better if they kept off the cuddly toys as Becky had said in the unit.

Today I'm driven to an office. We sit in a room marked "interview".

They bring Suit Man. He's straight off a telly courtroom. He'd look better without the dandruff, but I suppose you can't have everything and, if he was better, he probably wouldn't get my case and he's obviously pretty pissed off with what he's been told. But he hasn't got cuddly toys.

'Harry says she doesn't think you can do it,' he says, looking at Cheap Case, who is called Harriet and likes to be called Harry. To which I say pfffff.

'Neil is our barrister,' Harry says as explanation, despite the fact that she's not even been brave enough to talk about courtrooms and lawyers before.

Neil is looking me over. I check his shoes.

'Well?' he asks, as though I would be able to guess what he means. Harry starts wittering with a 'What he means…' but Neil stops her, and they all stare at me. Although Cardy in the corner just looks like she's gone to her happy place (I see a therapist who has told me about happy places).

I haven't said anything yet. After an age of silence Neil shrugs and stands to leave.

'You want me to stand up in court and tell them what he did,' I blurt, because I want this to happen. I want Lester to be put in a dark hole for his forever, I want to find out what he did to Mum. I want to get out of pebbledash houses. I want to walk over heather and feel the wind and weather hit me. I want that forever.

And I think I must have told them all that because Neil has sat down, and he turns to Harry. 'She'll do.' And they all nod which makes me shiver because I think of nodding men in pig masks.

Things start to move more quickly although I find out slowly. The court case is next week. All the time I've been moved around they've been doing things. Not sure who "they" are but it's all fixed now. I was mixed excited about the court. I imagine having to stand in that box thing and swear to tell the truth and then be shouted at by a wig man who says I'm lying. That's what they do on *Law and Order*. Then someone gets shot or blown up. Can I do it? Can I talk about this with Lester in the courtroom?

But I don't have to, it's all going to be on video. I won't go into the court. I will be in another room with a camera and a microphone and watch things on a screen. I will get asked questions, but I won't see the defendants. We are back in the interview room again sitting across a desk. Cardy has gone for a wee.

'The what?' I ask Harry, who has become more friendly but still seems to feel that telling me anything real is too dangerous for me to handle. 'The people who have been charged with… with… this awful… crime,' she mutters.

'What, you mean Lester?'

'Ah, yes, Lester McGowan. He's one of the defendants. You won't have to look at him. They won't show him on the video.' She apologises in case she might have frightened me.

She hasn't, I'm puzzled. 'One of the defendants? How many are there?'

Harry studies papers and she's got a more expensive briefcase now. Thinking about that I imagine she only brought a cheap one to the secure unit in case someone pinched it. So, she's not as dopey as I thought.

'Two,' she replies, as though that's all she needs to say. It most definitely isn't all.

I stand with a look on my face which could be confused with murder. Harry's heard about my destruction of the first house. She's searching under the desk for the panic button. I know that all these interview rooms have them. Everyone must know that. You know what will happen. She presses it, and either it doesn't work and I kill her, or a whole pile of people and dogs turn up and beat me to death. Can't remember which film that was. I point to the wall. That's where the button is. Harry is sweating. Makes me think she should watch more films.

'And Carl Summers,' she bleats, and I see she hopes that will stop me.

'Garage?' I say, with my own panic starting to build.

'Eh?'

'Why's Garage a defendant?'

'Why do you call him garage?'

''Cos he works in a garage.' No, Molly, don't say 'stupid'.

'Oh.'

'Why's Garage a defendant?' I repeat.

She flicks at her papers. 'He was in it with the other man. Mr McGowan said he was in it with him.'

'He wasn't, he helped to get me out.' I slam my fist on the desk; Garage is my hero now.

Harry doesn't want to tell me any more but she can see I'm boiling over. 'They think they were both involved in the death...' Oh God, she can't say it.

'No, it was Lester who killed my mum.' I have a blank stare on my face. That was hard to say. Makes it definite. Makes me think about funerals. Has there been one? No one told me.

'Well, they've both been charged with murder and child...' she stops, lowers her voice to a whisper and hisses, 'sexual abuse.' And she looks like she feels she's committed some crime herself.

I rant. Tell her it's not true about Garage. She looks at her watch. Cardy returns. No more information. No one wants information from me, I am meant to just fit in with what they plan, and no surprises.

It's court tomorrow.

seventeen

Today I am wearing a good girl outfit which is about as different from a good girl outfit as it can be. I heard Neil, the barrister, shout, 'Make her look young,' down the phone when Harry and Cardy were talking about what I should wear to court. I understand having to look young, and I'm not sure the reason is very different. They want to use me; younger girls are easier to use. It is simply a different type of young.

So, I have a yellow tee with butterflies, tan-coloured leggings and of course a cardigan. Trainers, not flash. No handbag or lipstick; my hair is too short for a proper bun, but it's brushed back and scrunchied. It's a good look, average. Wouldn't have lasted long in secure.

We travel to the middle of London – Tube, bus, walk. It's a bright day. Weird, there are Christmas trees and lights. I'd forgotten Christmas. On the walk bit we are surrounded by old tall buildings. This does not look like a friendly place. This is not Dartmoor. It's a place to run from and hide. Not a part of London I've been to before. This is a serious part of the world.

The Old Bailey. It's the actual Old Bailey, as seen on TV. I recognise the street sign because they always zoom in on it, but the name plate says, "Central Criminal Court". I'm taken round the back but as we move a van arrives, blocking the road. Lester is pushed out in a wheelchair. Harry and my new Cardy-care worker – Julie – stop and stare. They should be watching me, I'm off. New Cardy can run, Julie catches me, I'm shaking. I didn't think that would happen. When I saw him, and it was only the back of his head and that was enough, a cold damp hand reached under my butterfly tee-shirt and slowly climbed up my back, clawing the life from me. Julie is holding me tight. Harry is asking if I need to go home, if I can't do this.

Molly, do it, I say to myself. *Forever will get you if you don't do this. Nat told you it would happen. Don't let it.* 'Let's go,' someone inside me says.

We go through a back door. There's a room marked "video interview". Inside I think of Lester's set-up room for the pigs. I'm told it's meant to be child-friendly. Which is just what Lester probably wanted, more pig-friendly. I ignore the teddy bears and cuddly toys. It's technology in here, a camera, microphone and big screen. If this is the high-tech end of the court, then it needs help. Stuff looks like it came from a car boot sale. There's a man struggling to get it to work. He's shouting into the microphone. 'Bill, Bill,' he calls and says words that Harry tells him he can't use with me being there.

He runs out, still shouting for Bill. He's back. We get static crackling. It doesn't work. We are moved to another room. Bill's room. This one is called "temporary". This is more child-friendly. It's empty except for a desk and a box which I swear is full of exhibits. Much more interesting. But the technology comes to life.

'You won't see anything until they ask you questions,' Harry explains confidently.

I'm thinking that anything could happen as the screen comes on and I see the court.

'Off, off,' Harry is near hysterical, as though she thinks I could be contaminated by what is up there.

Bill can't turn it off straight away. He's not quick on his feet and there is a tangle of wires which he trips over. On the screen it's just like the telly. Brown wood courtroom. I see Lester and cover my eyes before I remember I've been told that he can't see me. Although having been here for a few minutes I don't think Bill would know what is showing.

I see Lester's face. I don't want to see Lester's face, but I will not turn away. He's making this up. This wheelchair stuff. I can see that on his face. I have seen all sorts of Lester faces, including the frightened agora-whatsit face. This Lester face says smuggy. He's making this up. That doesn't frighten me, that makes me angry and I grip the chair tightly. The picture moves. We pan around the courtroom. I see the jury. No pig masks. There is someone in the courtroom who moves the camera, Bill says, getting up from the floor and making for the off switch. Before we get the blank screen, I see Garage. He's surrounded by small people. Actually, I suppose they are normal size, it's Garage's size that makes them small. I don't like the look on his face, it's confused. He looks bewildered. I don't want my Garage to look like that. We lose the picture.

I hadn't realised that we were near to the end of the trial. Most of the evidence has been given on previous court days – days I wasn't allowed to see. Quite a lot of my evidence was written down. They don't need me to talk about stuff the lawyers agree on, Neil tells me that. My burning down the house is agreed.

We are hearing odd words over the speakers. Bill says, if he switches the whole thing off, he may not get it to work again. Might be better if he stopped tripping over the wires. There's another blast of static. We've got picture and sound again and more Harry screeching to turn it off. There are two wigged men whispering something about Irene. She has given her evidence already. I wonder what she has said. Nothing good about me, I'm sure. The two men start talking about "the child".

'You going to go for it? Test her evidence? Tear her apart?' one says before I realise I must be the child.

'Have to,' he says, and looks like he will enjoy going for it, which I suppose means a lot of calling me a liar.

The judge comes in, they all stand. I am the only witness, a whole day for Molly. He tells them about the video. He reminds the lawyers that I am a child and that he will stop any questions that he doesn't like. Doesn't say whether he'll stop any of the answers he doesn't like. Molly has set her mind. I am Dartmoor Molly here now.

The judge's face fills our screen, and he is talking to me. He removes his wig when he does and gives me a friendly smile. He's okay, looks the part, feels okay by me. He tries out a few of the Harry idiot questions about me being all right and finding something to play with in the video room. I want to ask if I can play with the exhibits box, but I don't and just mumble, 'Yes'. He tells me I have to tell the truth, or I will burn in hell – not. I don't have to swear on anything. So that means I can lie, doesn't it?

We are on.

The camera goes onto Neil. He looks great in a wig and the gown must be new on because there's no dandruff.

'Are you Molly Swinburne?' he asks.

I nod slowly because it's a long time since the Swinburne bit has been used, not sure where we got it from either. Nodding is not enough, he tells me. I have to give an answer.

'Yes,' I squeak.

Neil is warming me up. He wants louder. I give him a 'yes' too loud, more static, howls from the other end. The judge is back to telling Bill to get it fixed, he's lost the smile. Bill says this always happens. The judge tries to calm himself. Can't be easy if this always happens. The judge tells me to do my best. This technology mess-up makes me feel much better. I'm sure I saw a funny film about a court. Perhaps they filmed it here. That's something to hang on to.

Bill gets it sort of fixed and Neil takes me through more questions that are meant to be simple but include me having to tell bits of my life story which are a long way from simple and I'm still squeaking a lot. Then we get to it.

'So, Molly, I know this is going to be difficult for you.' How does he know? 'But could you tell the court what this man did to you?'

The shouting starts. The camera moves back to the other two men, who have to be lawyers for Lester and Garage. They're the ones doing the shouting. One says that Neil is leading the witness. The other is saying he should have said 'men' not just Lester. The judge tells them to shut up, well not exactly but that's what he meant. They go all huffy puffy like disturbed hens but do sit down eventually.

'Well Molly?' Neil starts again.

I am silent for just one second, and it is only one. Because I know what I am going to say. I have done most of this with Shanna in the secure unit. I do not need to be reminded. I give them the lot. Everything. I start from the day we got back to his house. I tell them exactly and everything he did to me, what he made me do, what he made me wear, what he made me say. I tell them all the details for every day it happened. I told them about the pain from the beatings. I told them about each part of my body that he hurt, damaged, and worse. I have all the words; Nat and the other London women taught us all the words.

A few minutes into this one of the lawyers tries to stop me, but the judge actually shouts at him and I go on and on and on. There is complete silence from the other end, mostly. Sometimes I hear a sob which could have come from the jury. I think that was when I talked about the blood.

I tell all the things I had wanted to forget. But none of it has disappeared from my mind, not one day, not one painful second of Lester trying to take the real girl away from inside of me. Nat said you will always remember. 'Remembering is what makes you hate everything; you have to hate everything because you'll never be able to get at anyone who does this to you.'

But now I have. At the end I am wet with sweat and my voice is fading. I stop. The camera pans around the courtroom. It looks as though they have just been watching another one of those movies where everyone gets chopped up. The jury are exhausted and sprawled across the benches, red-eyed, but their faces tell me of their anger.

The judge wipes his hand across his eyes before asking the lawyers if they want to ask questions. This is when they call me a liar, isn't it? They don't. No one is up to that job in this courtroom. The lawyers are not going to 'go for it' as they said before. I have shut them up, Molly has shut them up.

That's when Lester leaps out of his wheelchair and starts screaming.

'That slag, she made me do it, tell her, make her tell you she did it,' Lester is standing over his lawyer. He stops, looks like he's suddenly realised he's blown it.

Someone shoves him back to a seat, quickly. The wheelchair is removed; he won't get another chance to pretend. The jury has stirred. One man looked as though he might actually be ready to help, with his fists tightly clenched. I hear loud voices.

The judge is talking. And he does call for 'SILENCE'. Then he calls for a break. Calls to let me go away. He comes back on full screen to thank me.

'Can I just say one more thing?' I shake with my words. He doesn't look too pleased. A quite loud moan comes from the whole courtroom. Behind me Julie and Harry have disappeared. Bill is back on the floor with his head in his hands, but he's a bit deaf and I think the technology for him is more of a worry.

'Not sure if we can take it,' the judge says. 'But go on.'

'Garage – I think you call him Mr Summers – was the one who saved me.' I have tears in my eyes as I tell the court how he got me out of the house. I make it better than it was. Garage is my hero; how dare they call him a defendant.

Then it's over. We go back by taxi. Me and Harry and Julie in the back of a taxi. I think they have run out of tissues and can't face the bus.

'You did it, Molly.' Harry gives me a hug as we reach another new home, which is red brick.

Then she does what I knew would happen. She takes my new foster parents into the kitchen and talks. I am left with Julie, who I find is even more soggy than the Cardy before. Harry will explain just how poor a girl I really am, so much more poor thing than they had even imagined. I have been so brave in court, but now they must look at me properly as the poor victim, the damaged goods.

'Of course, it wasn't your fault.' I imagine Nat's words in my head. They are my words now. 'Not your fault that you let the Lester man do all those things to you, couldn't have stopped him, could you? That's the truth. It's just that everyone else will imagine it happening when they look at you. They won't like being reminded of the disgusting stuff. They don't like being reminded by you. They won't like you for it. They won't like you.'

But Nat hasn't finished.

'And it will be the same every time you look in the mirror. That's the person you really won't like. And that person is with you forever.'

eighteen

I am moved on. A house that's not brick and not white but just a bit muddy-coloured. I think it will be painted white after the mud gets muckier. Not something I want to spend time thinking about, but there's not much else now the trial is over.

I had a few more days of Julie and Harry. For them it was over, clearing-up time. They were just with me for the trial, and they didn't make a great job of that, did they? Running off and leaving me with Bill and the failing technology in the middle of my giving evidence. I think they hoped I hadn't noticed. And they definitely were happier to pass me on to someone else. This might not be permanent, but the new foster home was somewhere I could stay for a while.

'Providing she behaves,' muttered my next Cardy-care person who is going to be my long-term care worker. 'Providing she behaves.' Which seemed to be a catchphrase of hers. She's a busy woman, always busy with something else.

It's Christmas. I wake up late. This is like a bad TV drama, no speech, just mimed. My foster family do Christmas for me. The tree in the corner has lights and a sadness I don't understand. I get a jumper. We eat turkey. It's not exactly chicken nuggets but close. It's all over in a hurry.

Mrs Foster makes it to teatime before she bursts into tears and runs from the telly.

Mr Foster sits but has a heart attack face.

The doorbell rings and Julie has been sent back to me for this special day, to take me out for a walk, snowballs if there had been snow. It's respite for the Fosters.

'Their son died,' Julie explains. 'One Christmas, there was a car crash.'

We go back after the walk and I hide in my room, hiding for the next few days. Things get dropped in the kitchen, but they hold it together. Families are hard to understand. Seems like my view of anything approaching a perfect life doesn't exist, not much sign of any life.

I wonder what this foster family want from me. I think the answer is nothing. That probably means my not being here. They need the money from fostering, but life has fallen apart for them after the car crash. If I was normal, I suppose I should give them a hug. But I'm not. I am much too scared to think of hugging anyone, you just don't know what a hug might lead to. I do know.

There is talk about school. Busy-Cardy wears a jumper. She frowns badly when I use that nickname and I'm told to call her Joan.

'Whatever,' I huff because I think I should move towards being a grumpy teenager. I'm sure I have had at least one birthday during the Lester time. In Mum's timescale I would be going backwards, something like eight now. I know it should be obvious. Easy to know how old you are. You just look on your birth certificate, check the date. Which birth certificate?

In the middle of the questions someone had asked where I came from. Another easy question which shouldn't be painful. I came from a street, didn't you know that? I lived there with my mum, grandmother and an aunt. I went to a school called… ah, now we hit a tiny problem. I can't remember the name. Did I mention that everyone I knew is probably dead? And the street? No chance. The town? You want map coordinates? I know about them, they are on my map of Dartmoor, were on my map of Dartmoor. I'm sure I have stayed in Manchester, haven't I? All the Cardy-people said they'd check. No one came back to me on the subject of who, where, when. They talked about me having an X-ray to find out how old I was. I didn't know I had my age written inside of me. Like rock, and I suddenly remember sticks of rock, just not the scenery behind the rock, would it have been the seaside?

I have had birthdays. Sometimes quite close together. Mum said happy birthday, but it wasn't always the same time of year and the offer of a drag on her spliff wasn't the best present. Having birthdays was a sort of ritual in the places we stayed, a ritual to pretend that something normal was happening.

'Whatever.' I am on repeat to nearly all the questions now. I also do this because it's what Joan expects, she expects me to be grumpy. She expects trouble and you don't need a crystal ball for that.

I want to hear what happened at the trial. I've been asking every day and getting the stupid child version.

'You'll be an old lady before he gets out,' is the best anyone wants to give me about the sentence.

I don't accept that. I don't know how to make them tell me more except by kicking off and smashing things. I don't want to do that. I really want to leave that behind. I hadn't realised that whatever was going on hadn't finished. The court needed all sorts of reports and medical stuff before they finished. I suppose they thought I wouldn't understand that. In the end Harry was brought back to tell me.

'The jury would have gone for hanging after your evidence.' Harry is trying to cheer me along. I keep quiet. There is something I want to know; keep still Molly, wait.

Harry explains that Lester was found guilty of manslaughter of my mother.

'Not murder?' I can't keep quiet. I am an expert on crimes, on TV. Manslaughter is the one that makes everyone on *Crime and Punishment* start shouting and saying that it isn't enough, should be murder. Why isn't Lester being punished for murder?

Harry really doesn't want to tell me about this, and she blunders around with stupid words. That makes me braver with my questions. Eventually I think I got the truth.

Lester dumped my mother in a ditch. He told the court she wasn't dead then. He had said she was fine when he left her, but the court believed me when I said he'd hit her with the poker. But there wasn't enough evidence to prove he had actually murdered her in the ditch – so, manslaughter. Lester was given a prison sentence for that and another for what he did to me.

'It adds up to forty years.' Harry gave a puff and expected me to accept that.

I didn't. 'Last time he went to prison he got out and came back.'

'Won't do that now,' Harry says.

'How do you know?' I whine because I can't put my worst fear into proper words.

Harry talks about conditions of the sentence and how he

can't get out and what the judge said about him not being allowed out. But it is not forever. Lester's not getting his forever in jail. It may be a long time, but he will get out in the end and that will be before I am a very old lady if I even make that. I start to plan, just in case. They are very bad plans and would hurt a lot. Nat would have been proud of my plans. They show how far down my mind can go on the route to my forever hating.

Harry looks like she's about to go.

'Garage,' I almost shout – whining is over.

'Mr Summers?' Harry puzzles. 'He got off.' Harry is thinking back. 'Pretty much anything you said would have happened. In the end the judge thanked him. Neil didn't like it because he wanted to win his prosecution for both of them.'

'But he didn't?'

'No, actually the jury clapped your garage man.'

Okay, I know that Garage is probably a very bad person. Probably tears people's arms off. But he is my Garage. He is better than my African army. He is nearly better than Dartmoor. I am happy he was let off. I am not so happy that both he and the moor are starting to slip away in my memories.

School talk moves on to school clothes and dates. Again, I'm not told of all the arrangements. If I had heard all the plans I would have run away earlier.

o

Joan takes me and leaves me with the head teacher. Great idea to make sure that within one millisecond the whole school knows about the new girl who is so special she has to come to assembly with the head teacher. The building shakes with whispers. I needn't have worried. There will be no need for whispers. The head teacher stands in front of the assembly and tells all of them that they have to be nice to me because I've been badly treated. She doesn't believe in hiding the truth, she just can't say sexual abuse and sticks to badly treated. I have used the time to spot where the red glass-covered boxes are attached to the walls.

After the assembly I am led away to my classroom. I am not going to remember this morning of lessons because I know there will be a break sometime. That's when they won't need to whisper. It comes. I am in the playground, a place that is not used for playing, just for torture. They don't whisper. They shout. They say 'I bet you were…' they run through all the things that Lester could have done to me, that Lester did to me. I run for the fire alarm and break the glass.

After the school is put back together, I am in the head's room on my own. Outside, the head and 'told you to behave' Joan are talking. This room is quite nice, painted a soothing green, beige clean carpet, photographs of success on the walls, and the school trophy on the head teacher's desk. I have time to study the trophy. It's got names of best pupils and the years they were best, on little silver-coloured labels stuck around the base, which is made of wood. The actual trophy is a huge swan, in glass. I am afraid you are reading my mind.

Outside they huff. Joan and the head come into the room and huff some more. They say they know I have been through a bad time, but I just can't do things like setting off the fire alarm.

I try a few 'buts' which do not penetrate. I think about tears, but they will not come. They will not come because I am starting to boil. 'Stay calm Molly,' I say to myself, while I glance around the room – there is no poker.

'We'll take you back to your classroom.' The head teacher is all sympathy and smiles. 'Give you another chance.'

Joan sees it but she's too slow. There is no poker or anything I can use. The trophy is heavy. I aimed for the window (think flying swan) but the trophy only makes it a few feet to smash on a radiator. It must have been made of special glass, that disintegrates into a zillion pieces.

o

I have another therapist. And another foster home; one day I promise myself I will go back and apologise for the damage I caused. No one was going to listen to my explanation of what went wrong at the school. More things had to be broken. I suppose they could have asked me for information, like they would do to a real person. Quite a lot of me thinks that's because they know exactly what happened, or at least could guess, but if I brought it out into the open then they would look guilty. The head would look bad for not having expected his nice school pupils to turn into wild scavenging beasts at break time. Not hard to guess, probably happened all the time. Probably did when the head went to school himself.

My therapist, Hilary this time, isn't bad, she's just seen a lot of children with my sort of forevers and I think she takes Nat's view that it's the only forever you'll get. So, Hilary isn't surprised by the damage. Hilary is at least a bit surprised about the head teacher telling the whole school in the assembly.

'He did what?' And Hilary almost laughed in a hysterical way.

My new home is in a different place. I am not going to be sent back to school this year. Someone will teach me things at home. There are no glass trophies here. I am sort of allowed to choose what I learn. And of course I choose maps and geography. We have lessons in a sitting room on faded rose-coloured comfy chairs, sometimes we move to the table in the kitchen, sometimes we go for walks. And we go to places all around the world. We look at maps in the library. The best maps for me have a lot of empty spaces. I hadn't realised that Dartmoor was a lot bigger than the old lady's map. There was a lot more moor, but we were a long way from the moor in this home which is in a place called Luton.

One day when the weather is changing from cold to less cold, my teacher, who is a woman called Smedley, suggested we could take a trip to London. 'To see some old maps.'

Smedley has worked out that maps are my drug. I will behave if you give me a map. It won't last because the maps are drawing me back to the moor. I need the space. I need to smell the heather and gorse – Smedley has told me the names of plants. I do want to go to London. I left quite a lot of myself behind there, in that room with the other kids and women. And Nat. I want to see Nat. I don't exactly tell Smedley that is why we are going to London.

Smedley takes me to places. The Tower of London, museums, the Eye. I stand in one of the glass boxes going round. Smedley says they are called gondolas.

'What's up?' she says as tears run down my face.

'It's so big.' I point. 'London's so big.' I choke on a sob.

Smedley's not meant to touch me, but she can't resist, and I get a hug. She thinks I cry for some childish reason, being lost or something. That's not the reason to cry; London is much too big to find Nat. I will never find Nat.

But I do.

The wheel brings us back to the ground and we set off to walk along the river. And there she is. Nat wrapped in a blanket. She has a dog, a sign and a tin for money. The sign says: "Please help me, I'm homeless".

Of course, it isn't my Nat. It's a different Nat, but I can't tell that until I get close up to her. 'Nat, Nat,' I say to the confused girl, who just asks for money. When I see it is someone different, I ask her if she knows Nat.

'Sure,' she says, shaking the money tin at me. She doesn't know Nat. She doesn't care about anything. I can smell the cannabis. I can see the faraway look of the stuff Mum used. She is not Nat, but she is reaching for her forever. Smedley leads me away, shaking. She doesn't ask me questions. Questions are for my therapist. We go and look at maps.

Smedley doesn't take me on any more trips. We have a lot of teaching to cover. I don't know anything about the internet, but I soon learn. I can find out stuff about all sorts of places. I search out Dartmoor and the Letterboxes, Africa and I look for my soldiers, and even reports of trials. I get friends who I don't know in places I would like to visit. I email them and send them pictures. Smedley tells me not to trust them. As if I would. No pictures of me. Smedley takes me back to maths and reading. She says I am not a lost cause. Perhaps we should go and have another look for Nat and then Smedley would know about lost causes.

nineteen

As summer arrives there is more talk that I'm not meant to hear, but I listen to every word. The not-meant-to-hear words are the only really important ones. I am to be sent to some kind of camp for the time that would be the school holidays if I were at school. I expect the worst, that it will go the same way as the school. I am wrong. I meet people I have met before. They send kids from secure to this place. It has a high fence around it. They say it's to protect us, stop any bogey men getting in and pestering us. Right? It's to stop us getting out and doing our own pestering, in a burglary sort of way. You learn a lot in secure.

I like the camp. It isn't Dartmoor but there is wild countryside all round. Before becoming a holiday camp, it was another secure but thought to be too much like one of those wartime prison camps. Still makes a nice place for a holiday, providing you watch yourself. It's all girls. They don't trust us with boys. There is plenty of time for talk and it is a competition for the worst. I mostly win but there are other girls with terrible tales of families and injuries and men. But most of the time we run around and climb things and jump in streams and make believe that we are having the real childhood that we missed.

When camp ends, I go to another home. I am to be sent to another school, another chance. I have told my therapist – who listens because she's paid to listen – and she promises to make sure the same doesn't happen at the next school. She's lying. I know she can't keep that promise. New home, new school, new Cardy-care person. I am forgetting all their names already. I think she's Cardy-care number four or is it five?

There will not be an announcement of my poor thing status. I am bribed to be good with clothes and things, even a small amount of pocket money. Having learnt that lying is now officially allowed, I promise to be good. It's a nice school. Called a middle school. You only stay there until you are thirteen. No older teenagers, they say that's good for me. They have decided I am twelve.

I join at the start of the New Year. There are lots of new pupils. We all get eyed over by the thirteen-year-olds, it's not unusual. It's ordinary. We do lessons, sports, a bit of fighting, bullying and it really is ordinary stuff. I am anonymous, if a bit odd, but even that isn't unusual. There's an order to it. One kid, Henry, believes he's top of the heap because his dad is on the governing board – don't know what that means but he says it's important. Henry often says his dad is important, which clearly implies he is as well. There's always competition for the top of the heap. Competition to be the worst. It's usual.

Cardy Four goes to the pub and chats during her time off. 'Met one of your teachers, says you're doing really well,' she reports back to me.

I squirm. She looks puzzled. I ask if many students have a Cardy person.

'She won't say anything.' It's Cardy's turn to squirm, flush, stammer.

Of course she won't. The teacher is a perfect secret keeper, she won't tell anyone the news that she has found out about "that girl", you know the one in the paper, the one who had that trial, the one...

I get one more ordinary school week before the teachers start to give me the poor thing treatment once more.

One more slightly less ordinary school week before Henry gets to hear. Henry who is looking for something to keep him at the top of his heap. To keep him and his friends right up there with the important people. I think his heap stinks like something you might find on a farm.

I hear them whispering. I do not think there will be many more school weeks, ordinary or otherwise. Forever is catching me at speed. I take a lesson from Lester, something from my foster home, by the fire, I have a poker in my school bag.

'So, you've done it then?' It starts.

Today there is a drizzly rain dampening the playground. It's after lunch. We have spare time. I am sheltering under a roof. I like being outside. Normally I keep in the widest open space. Today I am sheltering. It is a quiet spot, hidden. There are four of them.

'She's done it with some old bloke, it was on TV.' Henry gets the demanded laugh from his three mates. They are nervous.

'We want a picture of it,' Henry says, taking out his new phone and he doesn't stop but pushes me to the ground, I bump down on my school bag, it hurts, and the other three kids are on me, holding me down. They are well prepared.

'Tape,' Henry orders, and one wraps parcel tape over my mouth, I can't scream, breathing is difficult.

Henry is under my skirt, I wriggle, he gives me a Lester type of slap. It all comes back to me. Henry is Lester. He's pulled my knickers down and gets ready to take the pictures he will pass around to keep him on the heap top. The other three are not so into this. They are not holding me tightly enough. I am lying on my school bag; my hand is in it. Henry is kneeling in front of me, my bum is wet on the ground, but Henry is not Lester and he will not do this. I pull away and swing the poker with all the Dartmoor Molly strength.

I have broken his nose. There is blood everywhere. The other three jump up and run for it. Henry stumbles after them. He has dropped his phone. I pull the tape from my mouth and grab it. The playground is strangely quiet. I pull my clothes up. I need a little time to get round to the back of the building where there are bushes to scramble under. Now I can hear shouting. Teachers are calling my name. I crawl further into brambles. I need time with the phone.

I am not Henry's only victim. He and his three followers have been snapping pictures of girls' tits and bums for a while now. Henry is still a kid really, but he has discovered blackmail, I read the texts. With Henry ready to take pictures his password was cleared. I can see everything. Thank you Smedley I say as I send it all to my internet address. Thank you Smedley for everything you taught me.

'She's here.' I hear an angry shout.

o

Another head teacher's room without any glass trophies. I have been told to wait. They have called Cardy Four and they have called the police.

Outside the door the head is being shouted at by an angry man. Henry's dad, the school governor, is calling for my death or at least something like that. He is waving his fist at me. I hear snatches. I see his furious anger through the glass. I could be really scared, but I think of Garage. Henry's dad is small, rather pathetic, not scary at all. Not when I think of Garage.

'She's nearly killed my son… you knew what she was like… what sort of girl she was… yes, I know she was the victim but… did she lead him on? No smoke without fire… you should never have let her into this school.' And so it went on until the others arrived. Henry's dad wanted to come in as well, they wouldn't let him, but he and the policeman seem to know each other.

Cardy Four starts by saying that I am a poor thing and that has to be understood. The policeman says that this is a serious incident, a serious assault. The head teacher says this cannot be allowed to happen again. I am not yet asked to say anything. The phone is in my knickers – thought that was a good hiding place. The poker… oh God, I dropped it.

'We have the alleged weapon.' The policeman has it in a plastic evidence bag. They all stop and look at me. The policeman is unsure. I suppose he's worried about questioning a young poor thing like me. Probably has to have a policewoman. Amazing how I am getting to know all the rules. But outside Henry's dad is still calling for justice.

'Why did you do it?' Cardy Four, now to be called Miss Joseph, asks.

'He was trying to take pictures,' I mumble. Now I am scared because I don't feel I have anyone on my side. Henry's dad has started to frighten me because I think they are all on his side.

'Childish pranks,' says the head teacher, who sounds worried, she must guess what I mean.

'Couldn't you just tell him to stop?' The policeman sounds as though that would have been the easy thing to do, not to go and break a school governor's son's nose. 'And he's a police commissioner,' he mutters aside to the head, about another position that is in the possession of Henry's dad.

'Difficult with parcel tape across your mouth and your knickers down,' I say to a room in which the temperature shoots down and a chilly silence descends.

'Surely… you're not… couldn't,' the policeman is short of sensible words.

'Children make up things like that all the time,' says the head.

If that's the truth, if that is the sort of school where this happens all the time, then why did they ever send me here in the first place?

'Molly!' is all Miss Joseph can manage when she looks at me. I think she is expecting me to burst into flames. She's looking all around the room to see what damage I am about to do.

Very slowly I take the phone from my pants and push it over the table. Henry's dad has been watching through the glass, watching and shouting. He stops now. Henry's phone has a cover with skulls on it. Dad barges in. 'That's my son's phone, give it to me NOW.'

The phone is in the policeman's hand. In slow motion he flips the cover. It's still logged in. He sees the photographs then flips it closed and switches it off.

'Evidence,' he says, putting the phone into his pocket. I wish I believed him. He didn't use one of the evidence bags.

There is a lot more shouting. I am taken away. I do not go back to my foster house, it's to another 'secure'. I am more usual in this place, now I am no longer just a poor thing, now I am called a 'well what do you expect after that', a no smoke without fire sort of person. I may have a reason, but I am clearly one of the bad guys. We never see the phone again (thank you Smedley for explaining the internet).

I find out nothing until I am accused. Henry's dad is still after revenge. I am to be taken down to the police station, to be charged with assault. But I am computer Molly and I send the school a file from my cloud storage. I suggest that it could be sent to other people.

There is gasping, I can hear it.

I never see the police station again after that. Someone who says he is important comes to the secure unit and talks to me about computers. Although Smedley has taught me a lot, I don't know enough to stop this man removing everything that I have saved.

Nobody asks me any more questions.

Cardy says something will happen. 'He won't get away with it.'

No one in this secure believes anything will happen – and I am one of them.

Being important will save Henry and his dad, but it will not save me. They certainly have not made anything better for me.

Joan is back and she takes me away from secure.

I don't think Joan wanted to see me again. They are running out of replacements. Joan witters in the car as we head for another foster home, it is a long way. At least it is school holidays, so I won't have to destroy swans or anything for a while. Joan treats me differently. I may have had a good reason, but I still broke Henry's nose. Perhaps I have convinced them that I am no longer a poor thing at all. I am a dangerous thing, even though they will pretend that I am something different.

As Joan drives and witters even more, I feel something else is wrong. I think the next new home is going to be a problem. Joan is jittery, like Mum was when things were about to go particularly wrong – as opposed to ordinary wrong.

We arrive. The new foster home is in a row of houses opposite a green space that's called the Rec, which looks a good place for bad things, and I will stay away from it. We cross the front door and meet the F-Mum and F-Dad who seem okay, if a bit over-familiar with having foster kids, which is odd because Joan told me they weren't often used. There is another girl here, his stepdaughter. She's older and goes to a college. She had a wary look. We pass on the stairs, she slows. I think she'd like to say something to me, but she doesn't. I am shown to my room. I look for a lock on the door. There isn't one. This house is going to be a problem.

twenty

Surprising how quickly one moves from poor thing to damaged dangerous goods. With the first you get treated like an idiot with pathetic sympathy and the second you are treated like something infectious. I do not regret breaking the nose of that boy, but I do know the reputation it has given me is taking me so much closer to my forever. A few more trips to secure and I will be right there.

I am living in this new foster home and waiting for the thing to happen that I am expecting. My options could be limited to angry damage. I believe I will have to destroy this house. I think there will be more petrol in the garage.

I don't hear Nat's voice so much now; the new girl I saw in London has taken over. I will be her, give me a begging sign and a money tin. Looking out over this Rec space I can see exactly where I would get some chemical to take me further down that route. The Rec is a shopping mall for drugs. The F-people are calling me for tea.

The house is smart in a nervous way. The F-Mum is heavy with make-up and tidies like she is being inspected. The stepdaughter takes food on the run and gives me looks which

I would prefer not to understand, but I can't help this new skill of mine – understanding. F-Dad is at home. He reads the paper. He talks to me about world stuff. He asks me questions. He tries to be matey about my nose-breaking. His knee jostles me slightly, twice. I am looking around for things to break.

I take to my room. I understand. I can feel the understanding making my whole body tighten. I must look around – I feel that I am back in Lester's house. There are no plants crashing in the wind, just cheap flowery curtains at the windows. I stop outside the Step's door; it's shut tight with music that says keep out.

I have to do something. My room is small, but ready for me. I even have an old TV, but I don't need it. I have my own technology and it's not wired like Bill's courtroom mess. I have learnt more, how to protect myself, to hide in the web. I even think that it may be possible to get back my cloud storage.

I check my anonymous friends. I have every security feature on my side. My location services say I live in Chad (that's Africa), I went to university in Singapore and my favourite music is Bach (like the dog). It gets me strange messages from genuine weirdos, but you don't need to worry about trust. Molly, age range eight to twelve and a bit, fostered with history of violence would get me a different heap of internet friends. But now I do need to find out where I am which will take me from safety for a while as the GPS kicks in.

My room, like the rooms in secure, has the bolt on the outside.

It is on the second night that he comes in to check I am all right. This is not appropriate. I know that. Of course, it's not appropriate. F-Dad has the eyes of Lester. I know what he wants as he sits on the end of my bed and pats my leg through the covers. I have three options.

One: I scream and throw the TV through the window. If he is the man I think he is, he will hit me. Frightened F-Mum will not appear, she has more tidying to do and bruises to hide. Stepdaughter's music will be turned up and I will be told it's all my fault.

Two: I do a Nat and negotiate what this man wants for favours and money. Forever here I come.

I take option three. I have dreamt about using this.

'Nice of you to take me in,' I say with the voice of an angel. 'I'm just a bit worried about my period, can you help?'

And he leaves at speed. I wondered if he'd get his wife, but she doesn't appear. Probably because he won't tell her that he's been in my room. What happens in this house is not talked about. That is not all of my option three because I can't use that line too often and the rest of the option needs to wait until much later.

I pack. Not much but at least it's not the working clothes Mum packed for me last time we were on the run. I will have to be quiet. I lower the bag out of the window into a bush, no noise. I have planned this because this part of option three was going to happen even if F-Dad wasn't the Lester type.

I was going to leave anyway. I am Molly the brave, although the feeling in my tummy makes me wonder if I am actually starting a period. The internet has been very informative. If I ever found Nat there are some things I need to tell her because she got them wrong.

I creep downstairs. Molly the special agent avoids squeaky stair number five and goes through the kitchen. There is an eerie orange light from streetlamps outside, not bright enough to stop me banging into a chair, which squeaks on the vinyl floor. My stomach tightens again. I see Lester. I have to fight to keep my eyes open, remember to breathe. The back door is locked and bolted, top and bottom. This house makes noises, not like the one on Dartmoor; this is quite a new house but there are still noises – clicks and whirrs and shuffling. Each one brings me a Lester. The bolts slide, the key turns creakily. A door opens upstairs. Steps on the landing, they stop, I think he is at my bedroom door. If I run, they will catch me – option three is failing. They will lock me in. The footsteps move on. It's her, F-mum, going to the loo. The flush makes enough noise for me to slip through the door. I run across the Rec, there is no one here. As I run, I wonder if F-Mum knew, her toilet flush was a cover – for me. She couldn't save me if I had stayed.

Technology had shown me where I was, even if I had to be less anonymous by changing my location services.

The station, the bus, the roads. I am not an idiot. Bus or train from here will get me found. I will get found anyway but I have to get further away, option three. I walk. I am Molly the Dartmoor walker. I think I have about four hours before the next day gets going. I checked that on my watch which isn't Mickey Mouse, can't remember what happened to that, don't want to remember. I walk and hide from any car, but the streets are quiet. I have a jumper with a hood. Probably the cars wouldn't stop even if they saw me. But technology has found me a path off the road which runs to the next town. As daylight comes, I stop and change into my schoolgirl outfit. Might not be the right school for here, but who's checking, provided I get a train before it's completely full. Pupils on early trains are the bullied ones trying to avoid people, I will fit in. Technology has told me the train times.

Oh Molly! It's school holidays.

I push on but my legs feel weak. Option three needed

me to wait another month. Too late. I buy a ticket from the machine. It's a busy station even this early. I wait outside in another bush until I hear the announcement that the train is coming. I run and climb on board. Sit. Don't look around at men and women in suits going to work.

'Off to see my grandmother,' I mumble to one who plonks herself down next to me after the next station and asks questions.

'Oh where?' She's like a suspicious interrogator.

Should I say, a graveyard somewhere? Not a good idea. 'Bristol.' I pick because that is on this train line.

'Oh, hi Deirdre.'

I am saved as another plonky woman sits opposite. The two of them take off on an epic story of children, divorce, illness, plumbing (?) and, of course, men. I am not expected to join in. If I had I could have given them suggestions – but not about the plumbing. They get off at somewhere called a Parkway. By that time, I know a lot about them. Too much.

'Hope it goes well,' the first woman says as she leaves.

I look puzzled because I am phased out on their holiday problems.

'Your gran,' she says suspiciously. I nod. She has to get off the train. She will remember me.

The train goes on. It's quieter now, not going the right way to take people to work. We cross fields. The sea is in the distance. More towns, and then more people. I brought a book to hide behind. Found it in my room. It's about rabbits. I just stare at the pages. I don't like what they do, the rabbits I mean.

Exeter.

I walk as though I know where I am going. Which I do because I have studied my map and I'm good with maps.

Up the hill, past shops, to the bus station. I have a jumper which mostly covers my school outfit. The bus station is full of loudspeaker noise and beeping buses. I ask questions because it is impossible to find the right bus. Asking seems okay here. Doesn't seem strange to them that I should be on my own catching a bus.

There is a group of girls, on their own and not much older than me. We all get on the same bus. They are normal and happy. I listen to them. They are going for a walk – on my moor. I hear their excitement. Are they safe? I hear they are meeting someone – Miss Someone, maybe a teacher, it's a school holiday activity. I listen to their planned route on the moor, as we head out of the town. They have a map. I am desperate to look at it. I think I know a better route. Even though it is torture I don't say anything.

I get off with the girls at the bottom of a hill. I don't want to meet their teacher, so I head to the trees, the bushes, the path I know is there. I have come home. Up ahead the moor stretches for miles. The clouds are gathering. I walk on. Brambles scratch against me, I don't care. Nettles sting me; okay I do care and I've got wet feet. I may not be in some good girl outfit, but I need better boots. Will any of the boots have survived? Doubt there will be anything left.

Through the village, almost at a run.

The house has been rebuilt. The roof has new slates, the windows are clean, walls are a sparkling white, at least half of it. The trees and bushes have been cut back. It isn't a hidden lonely house anymore. The fire must have destroyed most of it. The bit that has been rebuilt. But at the side one part has survived, looks old, it just has to be...

I creep up to the back door, telling myself that Lester is in jail. He can't be here. The kitchen door is pretty much like the old one. Painted red and with no broken glass for me to use to get in. But the door is slightly open. I can hear someone inside. I move to get a glance. It's Irene.

I go straight in. This is my house now. Irene sees me or am I just someone in a hood coming through the door. I barge straight past her.

'Hey, what?' from her.

I don't stop and not a word from me. I almost run. The old part was not taken by the fire, the side part. It is almost the same. Irene hasn't changed it and hasn't done any painting here. I can still smell the smoke, patches of soot on the walls. The old lady's room is much the same. Bit tidier. The bed is there. I see flowers in a vase. I dump my bag on the floor, collapse on the bed. Irene is standing over me.

'What?' I say. She turns away. This is my room. Really is my room. I am home.

twenty-one

I think living with Irene will work if we don't talk. I fell asleep almost as soon as I hit the bed. I woke to find I had a pillow and a duvet covering me. Glass of water beside me.

'Nice bathroom,' I said, having used the loo.

'Can't stay here,' Irene tries to snarl at me.

'Can.' I look for food. Irene pushes me away, sits me down and after a while I get fish fingers, peas and chips. No chicken nuggets.

The room is very different but the same. Kitchen units on one side, table, chairs and unlit fire. All clean, tidy and nice. No poker.

'Can I look around?' I had thought of just doing it.

'Might as well.'

The house layout is the same. The ex-film candle room is white all over, you can see the moor now that the trees have been cut. It's the tops of the moor. I rush upstairs. Only one bedroom is used, not Mum's. The rest are empty. It looks like Irene moving in is still work in progress (nice phrase used by one of the Cardy workers about me).

I stare out of Irene's window at my moor. I see the flagpole, no flag today, no shooting. Further up are the rocks of the Tor, my Tor. Irene is standing behind me. She goes on about how difficult it was to get back into the house.

'Nearly a year,' she says, and I realise with the end of summer we are reaching one year since the fire, since... well since.

'After you burnt it down.' Irene is sounding falsely cross. 'Had to build it just the same, listed – see.'

'Eh.' That's all the words I'm managing. I need to get outside.

'Listed. This house is on a list of protected buildings. So I had to make it look the same.' She gives a frustrated sigh. 'Insurance paid in the end.'

We stand and look out. Better not to say anything. I turn and somehow we collide into a hug. There are tears from both of us; the hug doesn't find an end until we both slide to the floor.

'Can't stay,' she says again without the snarl.

'Can,' I repeat. I get up.

Downstairs in my end of the house – it is my end – there isn't much change. It needs tidying and this time I will do it, there are still boots and clothes. I change. The key is in the mended back door lock and I am soon out.

I run and howl and laugh and scream so loudly that the shaggy ponies almost walk away. They don't do a lot of moving. Irene appears again. Not sure I can take another hug. She leads me up the Tor, up to the rocks. I've seen them before, but Irene points to a stack of rocks below the top of the Tor. Nothing unusual but Irene stands at one side.

I look but I can't see anything. She points. I still can't see anything until I move right up. There's a small gap at ground level. I peer in. I can see light. Irene seems to want me to crawl in, so I do even though she may be about to murder me. I crawl forward and after a few feet I am into a cave space. It's large enough to stand and light comes through another crack higher up. You could live in this cave. It looks like someone has. There's a rolled-up lightweight camping mattress in one corner. A stove, a pan and a few other things. I turn back to the light and look out. I have to stand on tiptoe. Through the gap I can see the house and the gate. Now I understand and I crawl back out to Irene.

'That's where you were hiding?' I say and she nods. That's how she managed to see me leaving on my walks when Lester was still there. We wander back to the house together. I can't stay awake. I wonder why Irene showed me her hiding place and that's my last thought until I am wakened by the wind. No crashing branches, just the howling Dartmoor wind.

I get up and wander into the kitchen. Irene is watching the TV. It's new and stands to one side of the fire. She's watching the news. I am the news. I am poor thing, dangerous damaged goods and now girl missing.

'Can't stay here.'

'Can.'

It's not long before the phone rings. Irene has a landline because the mobile signal is pretty useless here. Irene shrugs her shoulders at me before she tells – and it is Cardy someone – tells them I am here. I guess there weren't really any other places I could have gone, either that or on the streets where they probably wouldn't have bothered to look.

'On their way,' she says, putting down the phone. 'They're sending someone from Exeter. She'll be here soon.'

I nod. Now I know why she showed me the cave. I look

around for stuff to take. Irene hands me a plastic bag; it's heavy. I turn and I'm off.

o

I settled down in Irene's cave. She must have been up here again while I was asleep. There are more things and a blanket. Quite cosy really. I keep a look out.

I hear the car, and it's not many minutes before I see Cardy Four outside the gate with Irene pointing in vague directions across the moor. Cardy doesn't look very interested in searching the moor for me. Actually, she probably isn't interested in searching anywhere for me. But others do search. All the rest of the day and into the night. Police, walking teams, dogs and two helicopters. Dartmoor rescue teams. I am surprised they don't find me. I sleep most of the night; it's a good blanket. I wake to the sound of more searching. I feel guilty about it, not very guilty. Maybe about the helicopters.

At the end of day two it goes quiet.

'They've gone, for now,' Irene comes up to tell me and we wander back.

They haven't. Cardy Four told us later that she smelt a rat. It made sense but there didn't seem to be many rats up here. It's the sort of thing she would say. She'd parked down the lane and came back just as I had joined Irene in the kitchen.

'Can't stay here,' Cardy echoed Irene's words.

'Can.' I'm ready to run again. It's dark outside and they'd never find me.

But I can stay. It's partly because, although they don't want to believe me, they take enough notice of my worries about the last F-Dad. They take more notice when I tell them to ask the stepdaughter and I guess they'll take even more notice after they do talk to her. Cardy talks about finding another foster home down here.

'Near your moor,' she says, because I've gone on about it for ages.

Eventually, actually quite quickly, she gives in. We are going to have meetings, assessments, visits, more interviews. Cardy mutters, when I am not listening, 'Nobody wants her,' as the real reason for leaving me here. And I know that's true and I know that is part of the forever I have come here to see if there can be any escape from. I am here because here I can put the moor in my head any time forever tries to creep up. When I think of Lester in this house the wild place outside takes him away. I had lots of practice doing that before. Especially after I have learnt what agoraphobia is and how Lester just can't take any wide-open space. Something about his childhood. I don't want to think about that, what made Lester into the thing he is. Because if you did then you'd probably find something very bad had happened to him and you might start to feel sympathy. Can't do that.

o

When the meetings are done and papers signed, I am officially signed off to live with Irene. She gets some money for having me, which is good because we are both broke. The Press people arrived here along with the moor searchers when I went missing. They ran the old Lester story. Irene got her picture in the paper and a bit more money for her side of the tale. My name and face were kept out of it because of some legal thing about my age and privacy. That meant everyone knew about me and posted stuff on the internet. Some hope of getting privacy and when – which I'm told has to happen – I go to school I will get the full headlights on the poor damaged violent escaping girl.

We have a little more time left in the school holiday. Everyone official has left us. Today I planned to walk to Steeperton, on my own in the old boots not destroyed by the fire. I walk all along the stream, stopping to throw sticks and chase them like I did before. I cross over the shallow ford and turn back again when I see the drier way is over towards Oke Tor. I go out of my way to look down to where I first met the African soldiers. It's all quiet there now. Then over to climb Steeperton and now I'm puffing, not fit, must get fitter. I have sandwiches at the top because Irene pops up from behind the observation post when I get there.

We walk back together. Irene fusses about in the kitchen. I fuss about in the bathroom. We do a lot of fussing about because it stops your mind. And what the last Cardy said is difficult to lose – no one wanted me. That is a very big black hole. Nat had said the same. I guess the girl I saw on the pavement near the London Eye would have said the same, no one wanted her. It isn't true, it's much much worse. I was wanted, saw it in the face, saw it in Lester's face. The only person who wanted me was Lester. And there's something in that which turns my gut, something I have to get rid of or Nat's forever is still coming. Being wanted is better than not being wanted. Even for that.

For the first time in what has to be years, I think about Mouse. I don't have any fluffy toys now, but Mouse is the thing that keeps those thoughts away. Strange that Lester could do all those things to me but chopping up Mouse seems to hurt me more today. I didn't tell the court about that, they'd had enough.

o

I am sitting concentrating on a map to clear my thoughts. Across the kitchen table Irene is not looking good despite the shepherd's pie we've eaten and the walk we've had – which were good things. Despite all that, it's hard not to think we are in Lester's kitchen. Irene has things on her mind. I said it was better when we don't talk but she gives it to me – bang bang bang.

'I was a shy girl,' she starts, and that's the nearest to any happiness I will hear.

Lester was the only boy who talked to her, took her out, used her and in the end made her marry him.

'He hit me,' Irene says with anger. 'Hit me until I agreed. Said he'd hurt Mum if I didn't marry him. Don't know why I even imagined it would get better afterwards.'

Sounds like Lester, I thought.

'He moved in here with me and Mum.' Irene has a whole toilet roll in front of her; she's planned to tell me a long and awful story. I have a feeling we might need more tissues.

'He just wanted a free house,' she goes on.

And it was downhill from there because it was possible to get lower. Lester wanted the worst thing in the world. He wanted children and Irene knew why; she'd found things.

'Pictures and worse.' Her chest heaves. I want her to stop. She won't. 'He met other men. They did it together.'

Piggies, I think.

'I did get pregnant.' Oh no. This is the point in her story that might even make me want to take my chances with F-parents, just to get away.

'Couldn't let him have the child.' We both sob. 'I... I got

rid of it… I had an… abortion.' She whispers the last word.

She goes on and I have to blank it out, it's too hard, she tells too much. You wouldn't tell a child about this; you'd only tell a good girl who knew more about your ex-husband than she would ever want to know. I phase out. I am Bill on the courtroom floor with the wires and my head in my hands. I come round at the word "poker".

'I told him I'd gone to hospital for a cyst or something. He didn't believe it. Made me tell him. He took that poker to me.' She's pointing to a blank wall, but we both share knowledge of the poker's place. 'I was in hospital for months.'

I need the loo, can't go, she doesn't stop.

'While I was in hospital, he turned on Mum, made her ill with something. Then pushed her down the stairs. She did end up in hospital. He said she was a daft old lady and not safe. She never came home again.'

So at least she's not buried in the garden. Odd that I had never wanted to find out the truth.

'When I got out, I stayed away, hoping he'd clear out. I watched him.'

'From the cave?' I wondered how long she had been there.

'There and with a friend sometimes.'

Then I had come along. She looks up at me, dabs her eyes with the last of the toilet roll and says, 'Sorry about the slapping.'

I had forgotten the night of the fire. She's finished. It's better when we don't talk.

twenty-two

There are things to do. Things that have to be done to me. I still do have a social worker – down here, where they wear warm fleeces not cardigans – and there is some money to buy me more clothes. And I have to have a therapist.

Fleecy drives me, okay her name is Wendy or something, but I do not intend to get close to her. There's something on her mind as we drive. Has to be something about the therapist.

'There is only one who can see you,' she apologises. 'Has to be a man, but Sam is really nice and special.'

That takes time to sink in. We are driving along the dual carriageway. I'm in the back and if I strain round I can see Cosdon starting to disappear in the distance. It's almost bright purple. A huge beautiful purple dome of a hill. I look away and think about this man called Sam.

The other therapists have all been women. They've all had a pile of papers about me. Apparently, what I said at the trial was recorded and someone took the trouble to type it all out. I wasn't asked if it was all right, nobody asks me questions like that, and they hand the papers round to all the therapists. Each one – there have been three, actually four – obviously find it hard to believe. They talk about something they call false memories and ask me if I had heard about this sort of thing before, might have started to believe it happened to me.

I get annoyed. Especially when they talk about "this sort of thing". So just to check they take me through it. It's the "who put what where" talk again. I'm pretty sure I know. I'm absolutely sure I don't want it in my head. I stop talking. The therapists have all asked me if that's because it isn't actually true. I cry. They say it is all right and sometimes making things up when you're in difficulty is all right. For the first three therapists I could find something on their desk to break, hurl across the room, things to stamp on, glasses of water to smash.

For the last one I didn't do that. I told her about not being able to go to the toilet because it hurt, about the blood from somewhere running down my legs and why I threw up a lot. And I told her exactly what Lester did to me to make those things happen. And I told her again when she looked at me with her mouth open. And I told her again when she shut her mouth. And I didn't see her again.

Fleecy's words have sunk in. Apart from Garage, who has now become Saint Garage, the only men I have met have been the ones Mum found, the ones who came to the London house and Lester. If you ask me I would find it hard to tell them apart, even if they didn't all have pig masks. All the same. All wanting pretty much the same sort of thing.

Now another man is going to read all about me and take me over the false memory questions and give me the who-put-what-where talk. It makes me shiver. Will he just talk, or will he want to do some of those things just to check? Is that what men do?

We arrive in town, at an old building; his office is in a

psychiatric hospital. I look for people in straightjackets or at least white gowns. I'm looking for zombies. You have zombies in psychiatric hospitals in films. Perhaps this Sam is a zombie.

I sit on a chair waiting to be called. Everything in the waiting room is nailed to the floor. There is nothing I can see which I could lift or throw. The zombies probably got here first.

Sam is thin and has one of those scratchy not-quite beards. Cute if you didn't imagine what he might want to do to you. We sit at the side of his desk. There are enough things to break. I think he sees me looking. There are no papers about me, but he tells me he has read them.

'I didn't make it up,' I say, crossing my arms and pulling myself into the smallest size I can manage.

'Didn't say you did.'

'It's what you think.'

'Oh, you can read minds as well?'

My head turns towards an old cup of coffee. He sees me looking and moves it. There's a picture on his desk, framed and glass, it will smash. He moves it away. I see it is a picture of Sam and another bloke. They are both in suits and hugging.

'You gay or something?' I say, with nastiness in my voice. I have a vision in my head of two Lesters doing it together.

'Or something?' Sam has a smile.

I know so very little. I know nothing about being gay, except what the men crossing my life have said. Somehow, they seemed to think that being gay was worse than what they do. If they are right, then it must be very, very bad.

'You don't like girls then?' I don't talk like this, but I copy the sort of sneer I have heard before. I don't like myself sneering, but I have no other model to follow.

'I do like girls.' He still has a sort of smile which is making sneering difficult; it's a calming sort of smile.

He picks up the photo and tells me about his partner, Joe, who is a farmer. He tells me about the farm. It's interesting.

I blurt out questions. 'What was it like, when you were at school, didn't they take the piss?' And more. He tells me. We only talk about him. After a while I realise that it only seems like we are talking about him. The questions I ask are really about me. We get to the end of the session and I haven't thrown anything.

'Will you come here again?' he says, as we stand.

I nod. Fleecy is waiting outside to take me home. Something inside me feels a tiny bit easier. Home sounds a good word as well.

o

School starts next week. There is something I want to do before then. I tell Irene. She offers to drive me there, but I want to walk down to the village, where there is a place they repair cars – a garage.

The garage is blue and white and scruffy. My Garage is standing outside talking to two men, they are small. I want to be all calm and older about this, but I can't.

'GARAGE,' I scream as I hurtle towards this giant, running as fast as I can. I leap at him landing on his chest. It feels like I have hit a brick wall and I'm dazed, he grabs me, stops me from sliding down to the ground.

'Molly?' He says it as a question; surely he knows me?

He lowers me slowly to the ground. I turn and see the other two men. I have messed this up. My Garage may be my shining knight, but he can't actually be a very nice man, although I will always disagree. He wasn't having a friendly chat with these other men, who both look a long way from being nice. He was making a point. Having a small girl throw herself at him has made it difficult to be scary.

I see the other men smile. One says, 'She your little girl then?' And that sounds like he feels Garage isn't going to be a threat anymore. I have to save this.

'Are we going to tear their arms off?' I ask in a serious voice. If I hadn't been shaking, I was going to suggest I got the bolt cutters – seen that in a movie. It works. They are scared again. The men hand over money. Garage is happy. They leave.

I had come to see him to thank him for saving me. Strange but he seems to think it was me that saved him. 'Until you spoke up at that trial, they were going to do me for the same stuff as Lester.'

We don't talk for long. Not a lot in common. And he has cars to... well, I don't ask him about the pile of number plates... and other things that seem to need to be driven off quickly. He is still my Garage. I tell him that I am staying with Irene.

'You going to the school?' he asks, and I nod. There is only one school near here.

'My boy goes there too.'

Garage has a son?

'Lives with his mum,' he says to the question on my face. 'She and I don't get on.'

I wonder if there are many people still alive that don't get on with him, but there is something sad in his eyes. 'He's a good boy. He'll watch out for you.'

I walk back up the hill. I walk through the wood and smell

the wild garlic, more names learnt from Irene. She tells me things rather than talk to me. Therapist, Garage, Irene – I am almost humming as I walk. A shadow passes across the sun. This is not over, forever has not disappeared.

twenty-three

When Garage said his son went to the school it made me realise that I am in a small place. Irene drove me down to have a look at it. It's a big building in a small town and I will be going there. It was the school Irene went to. We stop at that because I don't want to know if Lester went there as well. Whether he might still have family in this area.

The term starts tomorrow. They say I am really twelve. My birthday was a few months ago. Irene and I found that out when we looked at my birth certificate. It's a copy and was sent by the social workers. I have no idea how they found it. It says my name is actually Samantha. We missed my birthday. Next year Irene says we will have a party.

'No, we won't.' I remind her about Lester's idea for a party with pigs.

I'm not having parties unless I have lost forever. Also, and I don't want to make anyone unhappy (yet), but it has to be a load of rubbish. Even I can tell this birth certificate isn't real. Check the registrar – Elizabeth Windsor. Enough said; don't think the Queen popped out to certify my birth.

There's other information about me in the stuff they sent,

less about me and more about the things I've missed, like injections and medical tests. I decide I will run with this, just not prepared to be called Samantha – and I do wonder what happened to that girl if she ever existed.

Appointments have been arranged. But I will have to face school first. Forever takes another step behind me. In a small place people know everything. Helicopter search girl arrives at her new school tomorrow, everyone will have read the headlines. They will have followed the trial before.

There is a bus that comes through the villages, picking me up from the last stop. It is half-full of frightened children and half-full of the children who are causing the fear. Everyone seems to know each other's names, but not mine yet. We leave the moor and head down into the small grey town where it drizzles. Always. The school is quite ordinary, lots of low buildings and tarmac.

The morning goes with forms and lists and timetables and meeting staff and finding the toilets and me checking the fire alarms, the escape routes and who to keep away from and trying not to listen to the whispers. Those whispers have settled on me after the first hour or two. We are sent for lunch in the school canteen. There are groups of pupils who know each other from times before. It feels like the room is getting larger and me smaller. The rest of my class are on another table, a separate group. Separate from me.

'Hi.' One girl brings her group over to me with their trays of something healthy, but below her tray she has hidden chocolate. They are older than me. She sits close, she's warm. But I wait for the words that will destroy my day here. I have no poker with me. If I come here again – which right now seems unlikely since I may have to get thrown out for my safety – I will need a weapon. The nearest fire alarm is too far.

'Jenna,' she smiles at me.

'Molly,' I croak.

'I know,' she says, but she says it softly, not like the threat I am expecting.

Then he comes in. It is not possible to talk, no one cannot notice, even the teachers. And he can only be one person. I feel he has to stoop to get under the door. He bumps a table by mistake, and it crumbles to the ground (well almost), the school speakers start a tune from some old black and white cowboy movie when the gunfight is about to start (should have) and there he is. The huge Son of Garage and he walks straight for me. The ground shakes, he doesn't. He actually walks straight for Jenna as the babble of noise returns to normal. Walks straight to Jenna, gives her a hug, sits, eats the chocolate from her tray and finally turns to me.

'Dad told me to look out for you,' he says, and makes my day. I am safe. Little Garage will make it safe. He picks up my tray and leads me over to the table with the rest of my class. Makes a space, there may be dead bodies. He sits me next to a boy called Rick. LG knows how things work, who is on top of our new heap; Rick is on top. LG whispers in his ear. Rick looks as though he's going to throw up. He doesn't. Rick is my new best friend, LG says so. Today I am safe, but I know that even LG can't protect me always, even if Rick prefers to be able to walk rather than be pushed in a chair. Today it is hard not to love the Garage family – not many other people do.

In the end it is not LG or Rick that keeps me safe. Jenna's sister, Elly, is in our class. Her group pull me in. There are no questions or photographs. I learn without those questions that other kids – normal ones whose mothers don't just work on the streets at night – those kids have problems too. On my first day I do not set off the fire alarm, nor on my second. I have enough trouble with the lessons. I have missed so much. More days and only small fights about ordinary stuff like food. I am given extra schoolwork.

o

Irene and I are good. We eat, sleep and watch the telly. We walk on the moor. We go further, sometimes driving to another part and walking for hours in a huge loop which I follow on one of my maps. We collect stamps from Letterboxes and have packed lunches. We even walk in the snow when it comes just before Christmas. I was invited by Elly for Christmas at their house, but I feel I must sit this one out with Irene, another toilet roll, and a downloaded movie about people who have problems that get solved. No presents this year or Christmas tree. We take bales of hay out for the ponies like her mother used to do.

Term starts again, finishes, starts, and so it goes. The school recruits walkers for the Ten Tors Challenge. I am now old enough to join. The walk is over two days on the moor. Lots of schools join in, maybe 3000 walking kids. I am in the youngest group – six of us from our school – we have to walk thirty-five miles and camp one night. There are training days, map days, equipment days. I keep my head down, not good to show that I know pretty much every stone on the moor. I do not want to be top of any heap. We get to spring and the day of the walk. The whole thing is run by the army from their camp. I am desperate to find Ivan, are my soldiers back? He's not there. We walk the route, to climb our ten tors. On the top of each one the army stamp your book to prove you've been there. No Ivan. Just rain and then hail and then snow.

'Lost,' says our top of the heap leader, Tom, as he looks at the snowflakes settling on his map.

'Why don't we try over there,' I point. 'Think it looks right.' And slowly I climb the next tor and the heap. Tom and the others seem okay about it. I lead gently, find a dryish spot on Great Mis Tor to camp. We do not get back to the finish before everyone else, but we do get back. A lot of other teams don't. I did hear helicopters. The snow was thicker on the second day, which was the best day of my life.

Two years later I do the forty-five-mile version of the walk. Still no Ivan. I am ordinary now. At home there are three of us. Irene moved in her friend. The one she sometimes stayed with when she wasn't hiding out and watching in the cave. We are a family. All girls, of course. Sam isn't the only gay person I know now, although I no longer go to see him. I'm not sure if that's because he thinks I'm cured or incurable.

twenty-four
forever

As my ordinariness goes on with time there is a question about my future. I am not some genius at school, I never really caught up. I am to take some course in geography, which I find is just as much about people as places. I still want to find the blank areas where no one lives but it seems less important. Many things seem less important. Possibly the moor is fading but I think that is because I do not need it to save me. In the house we talk more, Irene, her Lilly and me. Talk about the future.

I once tried a boyfriend. It didn't really work. Son of Garage heard I was going to meet up with the boy. He gave me the Garage phone number and said if there was any trouble he'd sort it. Difficult to have a date when you can always get his legs broken if it doesn't go well. Although I am not sure offering to take me to a football match would count as bad enough. The boy still walks but with someone else. My real trouble was working out what was expected of me. The physical stuff. I didn't know where I was expected to stop. It all felt a bit repulsive. I may be gay as well, it seems altogether more pleasant, better. I'd like feelings I could manage.

o

Back round the kitchen table again. Lilly makes tea. I'm looking at a map of Africa, Somalia actually. I think that's where the soldiers came from. I haven't found Ivan, no one at the camp knew anyone of his name, so possibly it was only a name for that training. Somalia looks interesting, Lilly says it's dangerous, Irene and I roll our eyes.

The phone rings. It's Garage. Garage never rings. Garage asks if he can come for coffee. Don't think Garage drinks coffee. We can guess why he is coming here. We have been expecting it to happen.

When Garage arrives, we move into the sitting room. Not a room I feel happy in and we don't use it much. I think Garage may have moved us, did he say something about it being bigger for him, more space? Garage talks about his son but he's looking at his watch. I am becoming nervous. I have a bad feeling. Should his son go to university? Big decision. Garage had done three terms in secure by the time he was his son's age.

Loud banging at the door. Garage is on his feet. 'Stay here,' he demands.

Irene and I are in his way. He looks puzzled. I point to the chair.

Garage shrugs his shoulders. 'I'm here when needed.'

More banging at the door. Could be the sound of breaking glass. Garage still wants to come with us.

This is for Irene and me. Better when we don't talk. She leads into the kitchen. There he is at the door; Lester is trying to get his hand through the broken glass. He sees us and snarls. So many things flood into my head. Lester, the only person who wanted me. The things he did. It is not real; he cannot be real. I am shaking as he gets in.

'Right, you two fucking bitches, I want my money and then you can get out of my house. Where's my poker?'

I thought we could do this. Irene and I against him, but I can't. I am shaking. He has brought back everything – I see my mum, stoned. I see his face and the twisted hatred mixed with his demands, demands for sex in whatever way he wants. I feel the blows. They have healed long ago but parts of my body feel damaged again.

'I said where's my fucking poker, oh this will do.' He picks up one of the chairs, smashes it down on the table, breaking off a club length of the leg. 'You get it first.' He points at me and steps forward with his arm raised.

I have no idea where it was kept. Where Irene hid it over the years. But right now, Lester's poker is in Irene's hand. I am about to get the table leg on my head. But I'm watching Irene. I feel she has the years of pain in her hand. She's fast.

'For my mother,' she screams, as she smashes the iron bar on Lester's knee, and he falls to the floor.

'For Molly.' She smashes the other knee.

'And for the baby.' Her hardest hit meets Lester's belly, fat from his last year in an open prison.

Garage is with us and takes the poker from her. I think he said, 'Not here,' but it's difficult to hear anything with the noise Lester is making as he rolls on the floor.

Garage takes no notice of the noise; he leans over Lester and seems to nod his head, after which the noise stops. Then he scoops up the unconscious figure. 'I'll take him to hospital,' he says as he pushes the kitchen door open and carries Lester from the room.

I throw up. Irene does the same. Lilly comes in and tuts.

'How?' I weep. 'I thought he was put away for years. How did he get here?' I'm shouting the same words over and over.

Irene says nothing as she heaves again over the sink. Lilly pushed her there.

Lilly has to rescue us. 'He got put into an open prison, Carl – your Garage – told me while we stayed in the other room. Carl found that out and heard that Lester was going to run and would come back here.'

I nod. Garage to the rescue. I just wished I had been strong enough to do what Irene did.

'Could have been worse,' Lilly says cheerfully. 'Lester was trying to get a gun. He asked the wrong person. Someone who passed that information straight to Carl.'

Irene turns. This is our second hug ever.

o

Two days later someone from the prison phones and tells us that Lester has escaped.

I hear Irene on the phone. 'That's terrible,' she says.

They said they were phoning to warn us in case he turned up at our door. And to let them know if he did.

'Of course, we will, straight away.' Irene's eyes glaze over, and I have to snatch the phone away before she starts screaming about incompetence.

I explain that Irene is a little upset (she has started giggling on the floor). The prison man says that he believes Lester has left the country. 'One of his associates told us.'

Ah, so Garage is now in the travel business. We hear no more about Lester, we hear no more of him at all. Garage is reassuring about that. I believe he took Lester to the same sort of hospital Mum went to, just a bit deeper in the ground and further away.

But now, for me, the spell is broken. Garage is still my shining knight, but I cannot be around him much longer. Now even Garage brings back Lester in my head. Lester's face will not leave me again. I suppose I am older now and he wouldn't be interested in me. The only person who wanted me wouldn't want me anymore. That should be good but somehow it feels painful. Staring out on the moor doesn't work either. Lester has finally ruined the place for me. I can only hope that one day the magic will return; it will not be soon.

There is something else. A couple of days later we are still a mess of weeping and laughing and howling and a bit of jumping up and down with Irene doing pretend poker hits on a pretend Lester – she's done what I wanted to do and haven't done. She's defeated Lester in her own forever. It is then I remember two things: Lester asking for his money which we haven't got and Irene's mum is not buried in the garden.

I get a spade from the shed. It's old and rusty. Gardening has not become a hobby for us. I take the other two to the place where I remember seeing broken ground. It was so soon after I arrived here with Mum. I only saw it once; it was soon covered up. I dig. We find the tin. It's not what you would call a fortune. It wouldn't have been enough for Lester to pay the money Mum stole. But it will help. Perhaps we should have given it to the police. Perhaps we should have given it to Garage. We didn't and we split it.

We split it because I will need it. I have followed up a lead with a charity. I will go to Somalia. It's a refugee organisation and it also helps young girls who have been "cut". The polite saying for female genital mutilation. I hope I can help.

I don't know what will happen there.

I don't know what will happen because I can no longer see forever.

ABOUT THE AUTHOR

Alex Mellanby is an author of a series of five books for young adults – The Tregarthur Series, Cillian Press (tregarthurseries.com). He has had a long a varied medical career from Hospital physician to Public Health, from the Seychelles to Devon. Those interactions with human distress promoted his writing and following characters through the worst of times.

 Matador